PARISIAN GHOSTS 1

# GHOSTS OF THE CATACOMBS

## JANNA RUTH

ISBN: 978-1-7386160-0-8 (eBook)

ISBN: 978-1-7386160-1-5 (Paperback)

# A NOTE ON SENSITIVE TOPICS

This is a book about ghosts, so naturally, death plays a rather big role. If you don't like spoilers and you're cool with anything, skip this note and start the book. If you'd like to be prepared, keep reading. I'm writing this because reading should be fun, not a bad surprise.

In this book, we dive deep into Alix's ghost-whisperer life. There is some discussion around mental health, in particular, a potential psychosis. That's the problem if no one else can see your ghosts. This leads to tension and quarrels within Alix's family.

Our heroine is also more curious than is good for her. For this book, that means a lot of crawling through very tight spaces, including depictions of mild claustrophobia, a panic attack, and stumbling across a gruesome murder before being chased with a gun.

As is expected in a ghost series, the nature of some characters' premature deaths will be revealed. Some scenes can be creepy or macabre, with cemeteries and mausoleums making a frequent appearance. A sinister organisation also disrespects the sanctity of death and experiments on corpses and skeletons alike, and they're also willing to protect their work by all means necessary.

The series will be full of action with physical altercations between the living and the dead, but our heroine is scrappy and will gain some strong supporters on her way.

Happy to tag along? Then join Alix on this ghostly adventure on the streets of Paris!

Love, Janna

# CHAPTER 1

I was seven years old when I encountered my first ghost. A few days prior, I had lost my beloved grandmother to a heart attack, and on that day, I was standing in the cemetery, watching her coffin being lowered into the earth, while a priest spoke words that were beyond my comprehension.

My grandmother was to be buried in Père Lachaise, Paris' biggest and most famous cemetery. You might think with all the celebrities interred there, there's no space for us mundane Parisians. Sure, the tourists flock here to visit Jim Morrison, Oscar Wilde, or Edith Piaf, but as long as you're a citizen of Paris, you can get buried here. It's what my grandmother had wanted.

The funeral was a small gathering. Just me, my sisters, our parents, and a few cousins whom I've seen only once or twice before. I don't remember much of my grandmother other than trips to the South of France and the smell of cinnamon. There's a memory or two about us baking together, but if you want to know what she was truly like, you'd have to ask my older sister Hélène, who was already ten and crying through the entire service.

My younger sister Odile was also crying, but she was a toddler and more likely to be crying because nobody was paying her attention. As for me, I remember not quite understanding what being dead really meant. My parents had tried to break the news to me gently, putting a lot of focus on how my grandmother would now be watching over me from somewhere else. I missed her, but I didn't understand why everyone was so sad if she'd just gone to a different, potentially even better place.

"What was she like?" The question came from a woman I'd never seen before when my father stepped forward to read his eulogy.

I knew right away that she didn't belong to us. Every one of my family was wearing dark, muted colours. Even we sisters had got brand-new black dresses for the occasion. Mine was a bit scratchy, but I've been told it was important to wear black to a funeral. This woman was sporting a bright turquoise blouse and a leaf-green skirt, paired with an orange scarf and prominent blue eyeshadow. It was all a bit garish, but she looked fun to me.

"Very nice, Madame," I said in a quiet voice, not wanting to draw attention while my father spoke, even though he took terribly long pauses between his words.

The woman scrunched up her nose. "Nice. Nice is boring. I asked you what she was like. Did she have any outlandish hobbies or an exciting affair?" Then she smiled down on me. "Oh, well, you probably wouldn't know anything about the latter."

I thought harder about my grandmother, trying to remember the fun stuff about her. "She once was a photographer. Some of her photos are black-and-white." I loved going through those old pictures. The people in them wore funny clothes and always seemed to have a grand old time. "And she loved frogs. There was a frog living in the drainpipe at her flat."

"Yes, dear." My mother had picked up on my talking and was absent-mindedly stroking my hair, which had been braided all around my head for the occasion. "It still does."

Emboldened, I continued, "One time, she burnt all the cookies, and we had to do them all over again. I got to eat cookie dough twice that day."

The woman laughed. It was a full belly laugh that seemed to be out of this world among the stifled sobs from the rest of the party. "Did she tell your parents?"

"No, it was our secret. She swore me to secrecy." That had been almost as exciting as getting a double portion of cookie dough.

"Who are you talking to?" my mother asked, glancing at me slightly irritated.

"To that woman over there." I pointed at my new friend with all the conviction of childhood.

My mother frowned as she stared right past where I pointed. "What woman?"

"The one with the orange scarf. Maman, can I have a scarf like that? It looks very chic." Maybe not in orange, but I liked how it stuck out at the side. It was pretty.

"Alix, sweetie." My mother sighed heavily and shifted Odile in her arms, who was attempting to wriggle out of the hold. "What are you talking about? There is no woman with an orange scarf. Now be quiet and listen to your father. It won't be long, I promise."

I didn't get why she claimed that the woman didn't exist. She hadn't moved at all and was standing right next to us. "What's your name?" I whispered.

"Beatrice Ileneuf," she answered with a warm smile.

Satisfied, I tugged my mother's sleeve and told her, "The woman says her name is Beatrice Ileneuf. Maybe she's another cousin."

"No..." My mother shook her head, once again looking right through Beatrice. Then her eyes widened.

"Do you see her now? She's very fancy."

"Darling, did you read that name from the tombstone?" my mother asked with a paper-thin voice.

Beatrice took a helpful step to the side so I could see the tombstone behind her. With me being seven, I'd already started school. My reading was far from perfect, but since I knew what I was looking for, the letters slipped into place. "In loving memory of

Beatrice Ileneuf." I glanced up at the woman. "You're dead?" A tombstone just like this one had been prepared for my grandmother.

Her smile was a bit sad when she nodded. "Yeah, but it's really not that bad, you know. Just a little lonely. Most people see right through you, you know? That's why I was hoping your grandmother would be an interesting plot neighbour. She sounds lovely, dear."

"I think she's dead, Maman."

My mother handed Odile to my father who'd just returned and went down on her knees in front of me. Then she enveloped me in her arms and pulled my head to her chest. "I know, sweetie." Then, as if I couldn't hear her when her face was turned away, she told my father, "We should've left them with the babysitter. Alix has started talking to the woman buried on the left of your mum."

"It'll be over soon," my father promised, his eyes brimming with tears. "Was it a nice ghost?" he asked, forcing a light-hearted tone.

Ghost. I mulled the word over. Until then, all the ghosts I'd encountered in my short life were the spooky bedsheet kind of ghosts that didn't truly exist. Beatrice was as tangible as the people around her. With her bright colours, she looked more alive than any of us. But if she was truly dead, then her being a ghost made sense. "Will grandma also be a ghost?"

"Sure," my father said in that inconsequential tone that he often used when he was too tired to explain something in more detail.

But this time, he was right. Like all the other inhabitants of Père Lachaise, my grandmother is now a ghost. She and Beatrice are the best of friends. A match made in heaven. Or whatever this kind of afterlife was called.

# CHAPTER 2

"This is so creepy," Gaby whispers, while her fingers dig into my arm.

We are both halfway through the catacombs, having reached the eerie displays of piled-up thigh bones topped by a row of skulls. I have to remind myself that these are the remains of the dead. The way the bones are carefully arrayed by type instead of by skeleton is somewhat absurd. This isn't a burial site, it's an economic storage unit.

Which is about right. Sometime in the late 18$^{th}$ century, after some cave-ins and associated health issues, the Paris authorities decided that the dead were suffocating Paris. They employed a fleet of gravediggers who worked for almost thirty years to excavate the bones and bring them here, where they were piled in these eerie heaps. It's a mass grave of unrivalled proportions—six million skeletons, all sorted by bone. And now it's an expensive tourist attraction.

My best friend Gaby came up with the idea of finally going where millions of tourists have gone before. It's because we're currently taking "The Enlightenment Period" in our first year Master of History. Going to the catacombs isn't a requisite, but sometimes history has to be felt—or at least examined up close.

"Which mastermind was it again that came up with the idea of stacking the remnants?" Gaby whispers, as if raising your voice underground was inappropriate.

"Charles Axel Guillaumot of the Quarry Inspection Department", I reply dryly. The bones don't faze me much. It's the ghosts around us that freak me out.

Gaby scrunches her nose. "Asshole."

"Oh, yeah." Storing the remnants of these poor souls had a disastrous effect on their appearances. By building this giant memorial, they're held in this plane of existence, but since some ghosts' heads might be hundreds of metres away from their legs, all those around me are either missing half their body or are terribly mismatched creatures.

I feel sorry for them at the same time as they gross me out. Normally ghosts are nearly indistinguishable from the living. I can even touch them, which has made for some very embarrassing scenes. Like when I didn't realise a person I spoke to was actually dead and talked loudly to myself in public.

Sadly, the ghosts don't care about the discomfort they cause me. Like bees to honey, they flock to me, basking in my acknowledgement of their existence. The same goes for the weird malformed spectres around me.

"Don't touch me!" Too late. A ghostly hand with only a thumb and a ring finger has reached out to grab my shoulder. The rest of the ghost is just as lacking. It doesn't even have a head, just some vertebrae sticking out from a severed neck. They were probably killed by the guillotine.

Gaby jerks away from me. "Sorry, I..."

"Not you." I don't mind Gaby holding onto me. At least she still has all her fingers.

Her face softens into a sigh. "You're seeing ghosts, aren't you?"

"In a mass grave? Never!" The power of sarcasm is strong in me today.

Most ghosts flock to their burial ground. It's where they are memorialised, after all. I don't claim to be a ghost expert, but from fourteen years of observational data, I've gathered that during their first years of ghostliness, ghosts might hang around their old stomping ground or beloved family members. Then slowly, the memory fades and all that's left is a tombstone in some cemetery—or a stack of bones underground.

For most people, cemeteries are quiet and peaceful—okay, perhaps not Père Lachaise with its throngs of tourists hanging around all the celebrity graves—but the majority of cemeteries are supposed to be deserted, solemn. When I visit one of Paris' necropolises, it's like stepping into a giant rave. Ghosts from all walks of life and all epochs mingle happily, chatting it up and forming new connections, often unlike any they ever would have pursued in life. My grandmother Eloise and her bestie Beatrice hold regular tea parties around their grave site, entertaining a huge variety of guests.

One time, they had a general over from Napoleon's trove. He told some of the most amazing stories. Don't judge me. I *am* a history student, after all.

Gaby shudders at the mention of ghosts. Even though she's known about my ability for two years, it still makes her uncomfortable. Thing is, she can't see or feel any of them, so she has to take everything I tell her at face value. As creepy as the ghosts can be for me, for her, it's a hundred times worse.

"I thought ghosts need to be remembered to exist," she whispers. "I know this is some sort of memorial, but no one remembers their names. Not even the people who dug them up did."

I try to ignore the throng of mismatched ghosts around me as I subtly move on in the hopes of ending this excursion sooner rather than later. "I think that's why they exist in the first place. The end of a ghostly existence is weird. It follows no rules that I can discern. I think they basically start forgetting themselves when no living person remembers them."

"Terrible." Gaby scrunches up your nose. "It's like Alzheimer's for ghosts."

"Yeah, I guess." There's a disturbing amount of headless ghosts here. Victims of the guillotine. "I think what happened to these ghosts was that they'd already started to fade away, forgotten under the city, but *then* some bright head decided to dig them all up and immortalise them here. So, now they're remembered forever, but not as the people they once were. I mean, look at it." I point at the rows of radial bones. "These don't even look like skeletons."

Right in front of me, a ghost has gotten their anatomy terribly wrong. The head is attached to a total of five thighbones with no rump or other limb in sight. It's so messed up I want to puke.

"Does it mean what I think it does?" Gaby's own discomfort seems to evaporate as she regards me with worry in her eyes. "They don't remember what a human is supposed to look like?"

I nod faintly.

She grabs my arm. "Let's get out of here."

With big strides, she pulls me past the displays of bones. As tight as the dark corridors are down here, I constantly bump into the malformed ghosts around me. They moan and protest, while I blurt out one pardon after the other.

One particularly bad collision knocks the head clean off a ghost. I flinch as the skull rolls across the ground, leaving behind a confused and disoriented ghost. "Gaby, stop!" I pull out of her grip and bend down to pick the head back up.

Luckily for me, there's enough memory attached to the skull, it feels like a proper head. The skin is firm and not much colder than

Gaby's hand down here. I try not to think about the fact that I'm holding a severed head in my hand. Sometimes, you need to detach from all of that—just like this head has from its owner.

It's the head of a man. Brown, wavy hair, not too unlike my own, frames his young face. He couldn't have been older than eighteen when he'd died. His eyes sparkle with excitement when they lock with mine. "Thanks for that."

I almost let go of him again. Picking up a head from the ground is bad enough without it starting to talk. Quickly, I turn around to where his body is stumbling around.

"No, no, please don't put me together with him again," the head begs.

"Him? You mean, it's not... yours?"

The head gasps, affronted. "That old fucker? Do I look like I have blotchy skin?"

Now, I see it as well. That body is at least fifty years older than the head, if it's even made up of only one other body.

"Do you know where yours is?" Though if I find his, I probably need to scour the catacombs for a new head as well. I quickly shut that train of thought down. I am *not* going to start sorting the bones down here.

Suddenly, Gaby laughs nervously. "What you're talking about? Of course, I know where we are. We just need to follow that path." She turns away from me to assure a pair of confused tourists. "It's quite the maze, isn't it?"

The tourists stutter something in grammatically horrifying French, making it clear they didn't understand a single word I'd just uttered to the air in my hands. Still, Gaby pulls me along, mortified by my erratic behaviour.

When we round a corner, she leans in to hiss at me, "Where the body is? Alix! You are not going to jigsaw puzzle in the catacombs."

"But the ghost—"

"—asked you to," Gaby snaps, then rolls her eyes. "It's one of those favours, right?"

I'm still holding the head in my hands, and he thinks it's a good idea to join our conversation. "Now that you mention it, I could use a favour. See, my bones have been scatt—"

I plop the head on the nearest headless ghost and wipe my hands. "You don't even know your own name."

"Alix!" Gaby's voice cracks sharply.

"Olivier," the head calls after me. "Or was it Jacques? Could've been Jean. There are a lot of Jeans around here."

I ignore the ghost for my own and Gaby's sanity. She's absolutely right. I will not attempt to match up body parts. For one, it will probably get me arrested and banned from the catacombs for life. And two, it'd be absolutely futile. I have to hope that Olivier-Jean-Jacques is happier with his new bones than he was with his old. After all, he and every part available to him died a long time ago.

Gaby races us through the rest of the catacombs as if she's suddenly realised she's late for a date. I apologise to tourists and ghosts alike. The former only frown at us, while the latter is calling out for me.

"My arm. I need my arm."

"Have you seen my left foot?"

"You've got to help me. He stole my torso! Look how he's flaunting my—"

"Flowers. Why does no one bring me flowers anymore?"

I glimpse a forlorn woman before she fades into the wall. Then we reach the gate that marks the exit from the catacombs. A few minutes later, we're out in the sunshine, leaving the ghosts and their multitude of requests behind us.

"Well, that was fun!" Gaby announces, puffing from the unexpected exercise. "I can't believe we paid twenty-seven euros to jog through the catacombs."

"I'll pay you back."

Gaby sighs. "Don't. I should've known better than to drag you through a mass grave."

"You don't need to watch out for me," I protest.

"Of course, I do." She hooks her arm into mine and continues to drag me away from the exit. "If I don't, you're going to burn yourself out fulfilling ghost errands." She huffs with indignation. "Sorting the bones in the catacombs, please."

"Not even a little bone?" I tease her.

Gaby bops my side. "Don't you dare!"

I laugh at the horror on her face. When she pouts, I quickly relent. "Okay, I won't pay you back your entry fee. But can I buy us a pair of pain au chocolat from the nearest bakery?"

"You may," Gaby says generously, the smile returning to her face. "Sunshine and chocolate are exactly what we need right now."

I wholeheartedly agree with her, but as we leave the inconspicuous exit of the catacombs on Rue Rémy Dumoncel behind, I can't help but feel sorry for all those displaced existences.

# CHAPTER 3

A fter fulfilling my promise to Gaby, I pick up my bicycle and ride to work. I've been fortunate enough to find a side job as a tour guide at the Panthéon. The national monument is located at the Place du Panthéon in the Quartier Latin, and technically, yet another necropolis. Though, while the catacombs are filled with half-remembered spectres of unknown identity, the inhabitants of the Panthéon are among the most distinguished and cherished ghosts. It's the home of the greatest people of France: the national heroes, the most mesmerising artists, and groundbreaking scientists.

Their ghosts will probably never suffer forgetting, their names and deeds immortalised in this temple. Being able to exist in their presence and speak to them is a historian's dream. But they mean more to me than just interesting subjects. These ghosts are my friends.

I'm barely through the doors when Jean-Jacques Rousseau accosts me. He's still wearing the curly wig and tight waistcoat that were fashionable in the 18<sup>th</sup> century, which he's been immortalised with in his official portraits, but he's kept his philosophy up to date, currently exploring theories of equity versus equality. "Welcome, Mademoiselle Alix. I need your thoughts on a theory that came to me last night when we were discussing Josephine Baker's childhood and how much, or rather how little the world has moved on from then."

"You know I can't talk here," I mutter from the corner of my mouth. The hall is full of tourists waiting in line or leaving the premises. I walk past the line and slip behind the counter. "Good afternoon, Philippe."

"You're on in eight minutes. Your group is already gathering." Philippe is the guy working the ticket booth most days. Though he claims this is just a stepping stone for him, he's been working full time at the Panthéon for as long as I've been here. "Full house today."

I sweep past him into the employee room to get ready for my tour. Rousseau follows me, not caring that the door closes through his face. "You don't need to talk. Listening is just fine. I'll ask your opinion later."

"Can't it wait?"

"Absolutely not."

I change into my tour guide uniform and adjust my name tag while Rousseau lectures me on the principles of equity I need to remember to grasp his new breakthrough. "And thus, when you ignore what Hobbes wrote in Leviathan and lean into—"

"Got to go." I grab a stack of brochures and leave poor Rousseau behind to meet my first group of the day. "Bonjour mesdames et messieurs, welcome to the Panthéon," I continue in English, since this group is an international. "I'm Alix, your tour guide for today. If you would please follow me."

As I lead them through the entrance, Rousseau continues presenting his theory, but I try my best to tune him out. He might still be a brilliant philosopher, but I'm not, and without me, his theories are mere whispers in the wind.

"King Louis XV had the Panthéon built between 1758 and 1790 as a church glorifying the monarchy. He died before the completion, and so did King Louis XVI. The National Assembly then voted to turn the Panthéon into a mausoleum for the extinguished citizens of France. The first inhabitant was the Comte de Mirabeau, Honoré Gabriel Riqueti, though his bones were removed a few years later." I've never bothered to find out where his ghost moved to. "Currently, there are seventy-five men and seven women interred in these walls, with our latest addition being Josephine Baker, the first non-French and Black person to receive this honour." I try not to smile at Josephine, who's wearing her scandalous banana-skirt outfit today. Certainly not appropriate attire for a tomb.

While I talk a little more about the history of the Panthéon, I lead my group upstairs into the gallery, from where we have a perfect view of the painting by Jean-Antoine Gros that stretches across the inside of the cupola. "In the middle, we have Saint Genevieve, our patron saint. She is surrounded by the Kings of France, starting with Clovis and Charlemagne," I point to the groups, "all the way to Louis XVI and Marie Antoinette in the clouds." The painting is incredibly detailed, with the kings and queens at Saint Genevieve's feet. It was commissioned by Louis XVIII after the restoration of the monarchy, and though I know certain inhabitants don't appreciate the monarchy throning over them, it's part of the whole package.

Once everyone has had their fill of the dome and the Foucault Pendulum within, we continue our tour along the resting places of its famous inhabitants, most of whom are anything but resting, instead adding their own odd details to my talk. It can be distracting at times, but I've had a lot of practice ignoring the ghosts, and sometimes I sprinkle the requisite tour material with their anecdotes.

"Supposedly, religious fanatics stole the remains of Voltaire—and Rousseau—in 1814 and threw them into a garbage heap, but that story is false. He is still in his tomb, as proven by an investigation in 1897." Had the investigation been able to see and speak to ghosts, they wouldn't have needed to open his tomb, because Voltaire is as settled in his resting place as one can be.

"I wouldn't have minded them getting rid of Rousseau," Voltaire declares boldly while shaking his fists at Rousseau. Unfortunately, their rivalry continued into death, and they have both made multiple cases about why the other doesn't deserve to stay.

Between the two of them, I managed to find out what truly happened in 1814, a discovery I can never hope to share with fellow historians since there is not the slightest of proof. But here it is: the fanatics *did* manage to break in—all sanctioned by the cleric—but there they were stopped by a brave custodian, who had switched the plaques of Voltaire and Rousseau with those of some lesser-known men. The fanatics buried those poor sods in lime, a burial fit for traitors, and their ghosts have since vanished, while Voltaire and Rousseau live on to continue their rivalry for all of eternity, much to my chagrin.

"Right ahead, Pierre and Marie Curie are interred." I keep a healthy distance from the pair of them. There is very little trace of radioactivity left in their bones, but their ghosts greatly enjoy the idea of radioactive glow. And knowing that ghosts are able to touch me, I refuse to find out how ghost radioactivity would affect my health.

At last, I turn to the place where I spend most of my time down here. "Our famous writers' alcove on the right: Alexandre Dumas, Emile Zola, and Victor Hugo." As usual, the three of them are discussing their recent ideas for books that will never be written, but they take a moment to nod at me.

Victor Hugo's gaze lingers a moment longer, and he smiles. "Hello, kid."

Of all the ghosts in the Panthéon, Victor is my favourite. He's a true friend and mentor to me after he sort of adopted me into the close-knit ghost community at the Panthéon, watching over me ever since.

I do my spiel, recounting the great deeds and even greater works the men and women down here have performed and created, peppering it with personal details that only a few people know. Victor always wants me to mention that he was conceived on top of a mountain on June 24, 1801, but I'm pretty sure he's the only one obsessed with his date of conception like that. He even put it into his grand opus "Les Misérables" as Jean Valjean's prisoner number, and because I love musicals, I will now never forget that date either. I wish all historical facts and dates came in catchy show tunes.

"When Hugo won his first writing competition in 1817, the judges refused to believe that he was only fifteen years old. As you know, it was only the beginning of his over six decades-spanning writing career. But Hugo was more than that." Like all the great people here, he was a writer, a humanitarian, and a politician. "He was voted into the National Assembly several times during his lifetime, and even expected them to offer him the leadership after

Napoleon III's rule and Hugo's return from exile. A thought he detested but was willing to take on for the people of France."

Victor glances up in annoyance. Even after all these years, he's still embarrassed about that misunderstanding. "It would've been a prudent course," he mumbles. No one ever said Victor Hugo was a humble soul.

I continue my tour by letting the people roam for a little and answering their questions. Rousseau continues laying out his theory, a constant buzz in my ear. "So, democracy is fundamentally opposed to the principle of equity. You cannot serve the majority's will while lifting up minorities. True equity requires selflessness and empathy and a willingness to listen, three things the majority sorely lacks."

"Here we go again." Voltaire is strolling over, saving me from having to abolish our democracy today. "All humans are incapable of acts of humanity. We are beasts and should be walking on all fours..."

I slip away from them, not relishing hearing their tired arguments again. After two hundred years, you'd think they'd have reconciled their differences, but no. They both value the other's intellect above any other, and hate each other even more for it. I guess I can be glad that Victor was born after both of them had died or there would be thrice the trouble.

After the first tour ends, two more await me. When I'm finally done, my throat is in dire need of some coffee, while my legs scream for a break. I take a respite upstairs in the staff room, where the likelihood of being bothered by a ghost at its least.

"Do you mind closing up again?" Philippe asks me as he collects his things from the locker. "I'm meeting friends at the opera, and we want to have dinner before."

"Yeah, sure." I try not to sound too enthusiastic, but I relax internally, knowing I won't have to make up an excuse for staying way beyond closing time. "Have fun at the opera."

As soon as he's gone, I check the Panthéon for any stragglers before locking the doors. The locks have barely clicked shut when the ghosts descend upon me.

"Mademoiselle Alix! A favour, please!"

"There's someone I want you to meet."

"Someone threw garbage behind my tomb!"

"There's a scratch on my plaque."

"I was here first."

The Panthéon has people overseeing the crypt and a cleaning staff, but neither can keep up with the ghosts' demands. I turn around patiently. "Everyone with damage to the right. Everyone with garbage to the left. Odd requests to the back."

Word has got out that I'm willing to help ghosts, so it's not just those entrusted to my care here, but ghosts from outside the Panthéon. I have a long list of damages to be fixed for the conservator—she groans every time she hears from me—and my own set of cleaning utensils to take care of the occasional littering and smudges. Those favours are easy. Others, however...

"Why haven't I been buried with my love?" an unknown ghost asks. "I bought the plot next to him. I took care of it all these years, and yet, they buried me outside the city. In the countryside! I don't want to roam empty streets and frighten foxes and bunnies. I belong in the city with the love of my life! We had plans."

I wonder if they had planned for this particular afterlife existence. "Look. I'm terribly sorry, but there's nothing I can do about it." It's strange enough that I can talk to these people. Advocating on their behalf with some bereaved relative is an absolute no-go.

"Please!" The ghost's face flickers, her will to stay in this place she doesn't belong wavering. "We only had so little time. He died before he hit thirty. I've waited all this time. He promised to be there. He—"

My shoulders drop as I sigh. "If you give me your names, I can look into it." Scour obituaries and follow up with family.

Her face lights up again. "Julien Cadeaux and Penelopé Feroulet. Thank you. Thank you so much."

I whip out my phone to take a note. There probably won't be much I can do for them. It's not my place to tell those left behind to dig up their mother's bones and reunite them with their father or whatever their relationship to the dead is. It's very likely Penelopé won't ever find her way back to the Panthéon to check, but I can't allow myself to think like that. The injury will remain, whether her ghost haunts me or not.

The thought triggers another memory, and I recall the displaced ghosts from my catacomb visit with Gaby. Their remains have been uplifted from their resting place and thrown somewhere that the living found more convenient. No one is advocating for them. No one even knows they suffer.

"Victor?" I ask as I wipe down the writer plaques. And yes, we're on first name basis. "Who do I have to ask if I want to learn about the catacombs?"

Victor Hugo knows pretty much every prominent ghost in existence, as he sees himself as a voice for the people... the ghost people, that is. He twists the buttons of his waistcoat and frowns at me. "As you might remember from my great novel, I have a modicum of catacomb knowledge myself."

"I know that." Any other answer would be an invitation to be thoroughly schooled. "But I was thinking of someone like Charles Axel Guillaumot or someone else involved in the decision to relocate the bones."

"What are you planning, kid?"

"Me?" My voice pitches slightly. "Nothing... yet."

Victor sighs. "Take this from someone who cares deeply about you, young lady. Don't get involved in catacomb politics."

I raise an eyebrow. "Catacomb politics?"

He waves me off. "The catacombs are a lawless place. Life there...
or afterlife there is unnatural. Wrong. No upstanding ghost would
ever be caught there." He strokes his waistcoat again, puffing his
chest out to let me know what an upstanding ghost should look
like.

"The people in the catacombs didn't have a choice. They were
simply uprooted and disassembled to fulfil some neurotic fantasy."
I shudder at the thought of what sorting the bones has done to
their ghostly existences. "Have you ever seen them? The disassembled ghosts?"

Victor looks at me with pity, but then his eyes harden. "A sorry
existence. Forgetting them would be the kindest thing you can do."

"That doesn't sound particularly kind."

He sighs again, exhausted this time. "Let it be, Alix. You're still
young. Go and enjoy life while you still have it. Let the catacombs
be."

Go and enjoy life, as if all I'm doing is looking for death. It's
advice I'm not hearing for the first time, and it only serves to make
me cranky. "Well, I can't do anything about it when I'm dead."

Victor Hugo has nothing to say to that. He simply shuts his
mouth and refuses to give me any leads. And perhaps he's right.
If the thought of how I can possibly bring together Penelopé Feroulet and her lover is giving me a headache, then getting the city of
Paris to relinquish the catacombs and give the people buried there
a proper and final send-off is asking for a full-blown migraine.

If only that were enough to stop me from trying.

# CHAPTER 4

The images in the catacombs haunted me all night long. In my dreams, I spoke to disembodied mouths, was grabbed by multiple arms all belonging to the same shoulder, and chased by mismatched lower bodies until I was buried under a mound of limbs and skulls. I woke up with my nightshirt clinging to my skin and shivering.

Even though it wasn't even five o'clock yet, I got up and took a long, warm shower until all the images were washed from my shoulders, played a little with my pet hedgehog, Malou, who never fails to improve my mood, and got out of the house as soon as the sun came up.

The latter helped the most. There's nothing like sunshine to wipe away all traces of ghostly nightmares. Not that ghosts don't exist in the sun. They do. They just aren't that scary in the daylight.

I ride my bike along the Seine, taking an unnecessary detour to enjoy the wind in my hair and the warm rays of the sun on my skin. At this morning hour, the streets are clogged with cars, and the bike paths are nearly as busy. Long lines are forming in front of the bakeries, the smell of fresh croissants hanging in the air. Many people prefer to take it slow. Instead of rushing into work, they meet in the numerous cafés along the river for a cup of coffee and a sweet breakfast.

Since I haven't had any breakfast yet, I make a mental note to grab a pain au chocolat from my favourite bakery on the other side of the river. It's not something I can afford every day, but if any day warrants baked goods, it's today. Chocolate and coffee should take care of the last nightmare images.

But when I arrive at the historic Latin Quarter that houses the Sorbonne, my favourite bakery, and the Panthéon, a different kind of nightmare awaits me. A crowd has gathered on the street corner with sirens wailing in the distance.

I get off my bike and push it to the other side of the road to circumvent the bulk of people. Some of them have their phones whipped out, which makes my stomach turn. It means an accident has occurred. Probably one of the gruesome sort, but these people have nothing better to do than to take pictures for their socials.

Only one person is standing on my side of the road, watching the proceedings with worry creasing his brow instead of sensationalism. It's a guy about my age with floppy brown hair brushed to the front. Some of it is sticking up, but a decent amount is falling into his eyes. He's got his arms crossed over the dark-coloured band shirt he's wearing and stares disapprovingly at the crowd on the other side, one headphone in his ear, the other dangling from his neck.

I feel a sort of kinship in the way he frowns at the gawkers. To be fair, we still can't completely avert our eyes either. "What happened?" I find myself asking.

"A cyclist got hit by a car," he says without looking at me. "One of those white delivery vans." He points to the van parked in the middle of the road.

"Ugh. They're the worst." Being a cyclist myself, I've learned to be wary of white vans. They just don't see cyclists as they rush through the city, turning without care. "Is it a bad one?"

He scratches his chin, and I notice his nails are painted black. "I didn't see it, but judging by that crowd, it looks like a serious accident." The ambulance has arrived, along with two police cars, and people are forced to back off now.

I sigh as they press into our direction. "It definitely makes you appreciate life, doesn't it?" I might be comfortable with ghosts in my life, but I'm not ready to become one yet.

"Oh yeah, most definitely." He turns toward me and shakes his hair out of his eyes before flashing me a smile. "I'm Gaspar. Sorry, we're meeting this way."

"Oh well, it can't be helped." I snort nervously. As awkward as it is, I tend to mostly meet new people at sites others would call morbid. Cemeteries, mausoleums, or memorials. "Alix Dubois."

"Enchantée." Under the long hair, his eyes are a deep chocolate brown that glint amber when the sunlight catches them. He didn't get to shave this morning, so a layer of stubble covers his chin. Something he seems to become acutely aware of, as he rubs his thumb over his chin. "Shall we get out of the way?"

If Gaby were here, she'd whisper into my ear that he's not really concerned with getting in the way and much more interested in spending more time with me. But for once, I don't need her to point out that somebody is flirting with me. Gaspar's smile is so infectious I feel like I'm walking on clouds. "Sure. I was going to get some breakfast at *Le Moulin*."

He pulls a face. "*Chambelland* is so much better." Before I can make sense of his sudden displeasure, he cracks a smile again. "I work there, so I have to say that."

I laugh, the sound washing away all thoughts of accidents and nightmares. "Do you do pains au chocolat?"

"Do we do pains au chocolat?" Gaspar asks in a high-pitched voice. "Are you trying to offend me?" For someone offended, he's sure grinning a lot. "Let me show you the best pains au chocolat in all of Paris."

*Chambelland* appears to be a little further away than my usual hang-out, but I follow Gaspar without ever second-guessing the decision. The bakery is in a corner house, facing a small square dotted with chairs belonging to either the bakery or the restaurant across the street. The line is rather small for this hour of the day, which doesn't fill me with confidence.

"If these aren't truly the best pains au chocolat…"

"Just get in line," Gaspar laughs, then calls out to the girl at the till. "Bonjour, Marie!"

She straight out ignores him, knitting her brows in irritation.

I raise my eyebrow at Gaspar, who grimaces. "She's mad because I talked her into taking my shift last night and now she's on again." I would be mad too. "Here, I'd better stay outside with your bike while you get your breakfast."

"You're not getting anything?"

"I already had a double."

Once again, I raise my eyebrows. He must not be much of a morning person if he's chugged that much caffeine before leaving home.

The line moves quickly, and contrary to the icy shoulder she gave Gaspar, Marie greets me with a friendly smile. I make my order and leave the bakery with a coffee and a pain au chocolat in hand to rejoin Gaspar.

He watches me with anticipation until I take my first bite. The best thing about it is that it's still warm. My teeth break through the buttery layers and sink into gooey chocolate, savouring the sweetness. "Oh gosh, I needed that."

"Did you?"

"I didn't sleep well." Flakes pepper my lips, and I raise a hand to wipe them off and hide my lack of elegance. "Sorry."

But if Gaspar noticed anything, he's polite enough to ignore it. "It's good, isn't it?"

"It's all right." I hold back intentionally and take a second bite. Yeah, it is good. I might have to reconsider my choice of bakery.

"So... you're a student at Sorbonne?" When I nod, he smiles. "How fortunate. Me too. What do you study?"

I swallow first this time before answering, "Dead people and ruined cities." I break the deadpan delivery with a giggle. "History. I've just started my master's."

Gaspar's grin widens. "That's so metal! I'm just a boring old sociologist. Well, I'm in my third year, so not really any sociologist yet."

"Sociology is cool." I can't help but notice that this means we're likely to run into each other at the library. The sociologists are right next door. "What's the big plan for afterwards?"

He groans, and I redden as I realise I just imitated my grandfather and his endless pestering. "If only I knew. Something that will help people, strengthen vulnerable communities, or maybe urban planning." Laughing, he breaks off. "I have no idea, and it scares the shit out of me. You've probably got it all figured out, right?"

"Yeah, that's why I decided to stay at uni and do another two years," I manage to deliver with a straight face a second before I burst into giggles. I just can't stop smiling in his presence. "Not really. At this point, I just want to study forever. Don't tell my parents that!" They've already made plans for when I finally move out of the apartment. "There's so much to learn, and it's all so interesting. I wish I could get paid for learning. So, I guess, research is a valid choice."

"I wish you could do my research. The semester has barely started, and I'm already inundated with work."

"Are you asking me for a study date?" I don't think I've ever been as forward before.

Gaspar's face splits into a wide grin. "How about tomorrow afternoon? I'll be in the library from one until... well until they throw me out."

I can't believe I'm doing this. "I'll find you after class." Having finished my pain au chocolat, I take the coffee in one hand and start pushing my bike with the other.

"It's a date." Gaspar walks beside me, still grinning.

"It's a date." Oh, gosh. It's a *date*. And I've set it up all by myself. Usually, Gaby drags me to some blind date, or one of my sisters pushes me toward some guy who's sure to like me. They all run when the next ghost grabs my attention.

Anxiety fills me as I watch Gaspar walk up the steps of the Sorbonne and vanish among the other students. We might have hit it off as if we've known each other for ages, but the moment I space out or talk to someone he can't see, things will sour. Perhaps I should skip the date and relish the memory of our chance meeting as it was.

*You need to put yourself out there,* I can hear Gaby in my mind. I sigh heavily. Time to find the real Gaby and distract myself with old bones. Yeah, I guess I *am* pretty metal. And even though Gaspar's not there anymore, he makes me smile yet again.

# CHAPTER 5

"You're in love."

"Excuse me?" I raise my eyebrows at Victor Hugo, who is standing over me with a contemplative expression.

Next to him, Voltaire is stroking the fabric of his jacket, while I'm on my knees at his tomb, picking trash out from the grate. Some idiot found it funny to empty a pocket's worth of lint, crumbs, and scraps behind the revered grave. How I hate tourists.

"Make sure you get the chewing gum from last time while you're at it," Voltaire orders, not interested in the conversation Victor has struck up.

I moan. "And you couldn't tell me that last time?" Chewing gum is the worst. Really, people have no respect.

"I'm a busy man, Mademoiselle Dubois." He finishes stroking his jacket, as if the ghostly fabric ever needed it, and readjusts his wig.

"You mean, busy drinking coffee?" A little-known fact about Voltaire is that he used to drink about forty cups a day in his lifetime, something he kept up after death. I'm half-convinced his eccentricity is due to the caffeine running in his veins instead of blood. Strictly proverbially speaking, since he has neither blood nor veins.

I lean into the cavity, using my phone to cast light into the corners. Sure enough, someone has stuck some chewing gum onto the backside of the stone. "Great."

While Voltaire proves an excellent distraction, Victor is not letting go. "What is your next step?"

"My next step?" I eye the offensive gum. "I will get my scraper out and hope my arm doesn't fall off, while I try to—"

"About the young man." Victor leans against the wall, taking great care he doesn't fall through, and throws me a withering glance. "You won't leave him hanging, will you?"

Heat crawls up my neck. Now that I'm no longer looking into Gaspar's eyes, his grin demanding a mirror image, my social anxiety has returned. "Look. It was fun, but as soon as he gets to know me better, he'll find me weird."

"I don't find you weird," Victor says promptly.

"I do," Voltaire chimes in. When I glare at him, he scoffs. "Don't get me wrong. I appreciate you very much, but it is not normal to spend all your time in dusty libraries and mausoleums when you could change the world."

Rolling my eyes at him, I reply, "I'm not trying to change the world. Most people don't." I get the scraper out, and push my arm through the gap until my wrist has enough leeway to get the work done.

"True. Otherwise, this place would be crowded."

Just once, I want to meet one of the greats who's learnt the meaning of humility. But he's right. It's highly unlikely I will ever earn my way into a tomb at the Panthéon. I'd better enjoy the time I've got with these ghosts while I'm still alive.

Victor heaves a big sigh. "You don't need to change the world. You're already doing plenty good just the way you are. And if this man comes to see it, he'll surely fall in love with you."

"It was one conversation." I get most of the chewing gum off with the first swipe, but the remnants prove quite resistant. "He's not in love with me, and I'm not in love with him."

He waves a hand. "I know that. But you always refuse to give love a shot. When I was your age, I was already married to the love of my life."

"The love of your life?" I ask, knowing all about Adèle. However... "What about Juliette?" Juliette was the mistress he kept around for most of his life. "Or all the other women?"

If he's bothered by me calling out his sexual adventures, Victor doesn't show it. To be fair, his wife had affairs of her own, one incredibly public one with a good friend of his. "You can't fault me for having lived a life of passion. I fell in love often and hard. I didn't hide from it as you do."

"I'm not hiding from love."

"Then why are you contemplating leaving that young man waiting in vain for you?"

You know you suck at life when a ghost calls you out. "It's different when I'm with you. You see them all, the living and the dead. Gaspar is just a normal man. The moment I get pulled into a conversation with a ghost, he'll most likely back off." The thought leaves a bitter aftertaste on my tongue.

"And what if he doesn't? Your friend Gabrielle didn't back off."

I sigh and relax my hand, which has started cramping from its awkward position. "Gaby was my best friend for years before I told her. And no," I stop Victor when he opens his mouth, "I'll not be able to be in a relationship with Gaspar for years before I tell him. I don't want to," I whisper.

Victor takes a deep breath, rubbing his beard. "You're scared. I get it. Love can do that, but take it from one who had a lot of experience with it. It's always worth going for it."

I highly doubt that. Victor's many documented relationships with women aren't exactly the kind of love I'm looking for. If it was that great, then why did the heroes in his story only ever fall for one girl? Despite my reservations, I want the love from his stories, not the messy reality. But messy is all I'm destined for with an affliction like mine.

Ignoring the sting of it, I return to my task. After a few more minutes, Voltaire's stone is as smooth as it has been since he was interred. I brush out the rest of the garbage and check everything before I crawl out of the alcove.

It's already past closing time and I'm the last one here. Perhaps Victor is right and I *am* hiding in here. Hiding behind dead bones and historic facts. It's no longer as cool as Gaspar made it sound.

"I will meet him," I decide on a whim. "It'll probably be nothing, but I will go."

"Good on you." Victor grants me a fatherly smile. "Give love a chance to sweep you away."

Always with the lyrical. "Yeah, let's get through a date first." I glance at my work. "All right. I should probably go if I want to make it home in time for dinner."

But when I make my way over to the office to grab my stuff, someone is already waiting for me. I can tell she's a ghost because her boots are encrusted with mud, but they don't leave a trace as she paces the length of the room. The woman looks rough, her clothes sturdy but stained, as if she spent her life crawling through dirt tunnels. She's sporting a side-cut and green hair that is swept over her head to hang on the left. The one ear I can see is heavily pierced.

Her eyes are deep brown, reminding me of Gaspar, but there's no smile to greet me. She stops her pacing to take me in. "Are you the ghost whisperer?" Before I can answer, she continues, "You must be, otherwise you wouldn't be staring like that. And you're not dead."

"I am not dead," I repeat, a little dumbfounded.

"Good. Stay that way. It's no fun being dead. Why did no one tell me it would be like this?"

"Like what?"

The woman picks up her pacing again. "I never believed in God or anything else, so I knew there would be no Paradise or Hell, but... unless this is Hell. Is this Hell?"

Slowly, I realise that her death must've been fairly recent. She's not the only ghost to come to me for spiritual advice, though I'm probably the last person who can give such advice. "It's not Hell, no. Just a different way of existence."

"To what purpose?"

For someone who never believed in a higher power, she sure needs it right now. "The same purpose as your previous existence. You just are."

"But what do I do?"

"I don't know. What did you do before?" My phone vibrates, but I ignore it. This ghost needs me right now.

She stops again, staring at me. For the first time, some of that nervous energy drops. "I was a tour guide." A mischievous glint enters her eyes. "In the catacombs."

"The catacombs?" Did I walk right past her on my visit? Probably, since I was a bit distracted by all the broken ghosts. "I'm a tour guide, too. Here at the Panthéon."

"Cute. But I don't do the same tours day in day out, spewing off some tired old script. I take people into the catacombs. They entrust their life to me." Pride makes her grow an inch. "I know the catacombs like the back of my hand, and never lost a single client." Then her confidence falters again. "Or perhaps not the back of my hand. I..." Her head snaps up. "I've heard you're in the business of helping ghosts. A ghost. That's what I am now."

I'm not sure if I should be offended because she insulted my line of work or intrigued, because she's clearly not talking about the part of the catacombs that's accessible to the public. "What do you want me to do?"

"I..." The woman stares at me. Her eyes glass over and she licks her lips. Then suddenly, she spins around. "Forget it. I should've never come to you. You're not one of us. Have a good day. Or night. It's all the same to me."

And before I can gather my wits enough to stop her, she's fled the office by simply sinking into the ground. My body tingles at the thought of what might lie beneath me. I've known about the catacombs under Paris for most of my life, but suddenly, I feel this urge to dig deeper. Of setting foot where no one is allowed to go.

I shake my head. I'm not a delinquent. The catacombs are closed off to the public for a reason. They're dangerous, a giant maze of crumbling stone. But oh, all that knowledge that must be stored down there.

With a longing sigh, I grab my bag and start to close everything down. It's just as well that the ghost left without roping me into another odd job. I've got enough on my plate without worrying about the catacombs.

I've barely entered my family's apartment when my older sister Hélène accosts me. "You're late."

"Late for what?" I ask as I take off my shoes and toss them onto the small rack next to the door. She's not even living here anymore. "I didn't even know you were coming."

Hélène rolls her eyes. She's an inch taller than me with a slightly more angular face, but could be my twin otherwise, if she didn't always wear business attire and her brown locks wrapped tightly in a bun. "You would've if you answered your phone."

Wondering what's got her panties in a twist, I follow her into our living room, which doubles as a dining room, the large table aligned with the TV, which is currently off. I find the whole family waiting for me, including Hélène's boyfriend Cédric. While everyone looks like they're already finished, an untouched plate of food is set out for me.

I kiss my parents and Cédric hello before squeezing into the chair next to my younger sister Odile. A glance across the table tells me that they've brought out the champagne. Proper champagne. But before I can ask about the occasion, Hélène slumps into the chair next to her boyfriend and glares at me. "You were supposed to be home by seven."

"Yes, Maman."

My actual mother shoots me a disapproving stare, but she has got one for my sister as well, so I feel justified in my petulance.

Hélène straightens her back and shakes off her irritation like the mature older sister that she always works so hard to be. "What I mean is that according to your work schedule, you should've already been home. What took you so long?"

"Just because the Panthéon closes at six doesn't mean I get off immediately. I don't just do tours, you know." What truly kept me were the ghosts, but I know better than to mention these.

My father gets up and takes my plate. "I'll warm this up for you." With three daughters, he learnt early when to flee the brewing sisterly quarrel. I love both my sisters to death, but with all three of us in a room, drama is never far away.

Hélène pouts. "Today was important."

"Why?" I say at the same time as my younger sister blurts, "Hélène and Cédric got engaged."

Hélène gasps, her ire switching to Odile now. "That's not your news to share."

Odile might be the youngest, but since hitting puberty she's stopped holding back and will do anything to claw her way to the top of the hierarchy. "Well, were you? You seemed too busy berating Alix for ruining your perfect moment to share it."

My brain is still catching up. "I'm sorry. I didn't plan to... Wait? You got engaged?" It's been less than half a year since the two of them moved in together.

Hélène leans back in her chair, crossing her arms in front of her chest. "Whatever. It's obviously not as important as I thought it would be."

"Léni..." my mother sighs, reaching out a hand to rub Hélène's.

"Take a breath, darling." Her boyfriend—no, fiancé—is a brave one. I suppose he must be, being a law enforcer and all. "Alix didn't mean to miss the announcement."

"I sent her a text that we're coming for dinner. And I called." And we're back to me.

I know better than to answer. Obviously, I missed that call, too busy to keep the unfamiliar ghost from freaking out too much. I bite my cheek to keep myself from explaining the dilemma, knowing it won't be appreciated.

"And she got held up. It's really not the end of the world." Cédric smiles at me, and everything inside of me wants to turn inside-out. I've yet to like a boyfriend of Hélène's, but this one I positively detest. He just acts so smarmy and superior all the time.

But I suppose that is exactly what she needs. "Would you like to show her the ring I got you?"

His words manage to loosen Hélène's shoulders. The sharp crease between her eyebrows smooths, and she leans over to kiss on his cheek. Then she stretches out her hand and presents the pear-shaped diamond ring on her finger. "Isn't it gorgeous?"

"Wow." I'm not a big fan of jewellery, and thus not much of an expert, but even I know that this ring must have cost a lot. "I didn't know the police paid this well."

Hélène lit up at my initial surprise, but her mood takes a dive again when she hears the rest of my reply. "Can't you just say how pretty it is?"

"So pretty!" Odile exclaims, her eyes twinkling in a way that makes me suspect she's not nearly as enamoured with it as she pretends to be.

Meanwhile, Cédric seems amused. "It took some time to save up." He leans back, his arm wrapping around my sister's shoulders. "But you're right, the pay isn't that bad either. Perhaps something to consider."

I stare at him dumbfounded, only breaking out of my stupor when my father places my plate back in front of me. "Why would I consider joining the police?" Does Cédric have a recruitment quota to fill? Why is he going after me of all people?

He leans forward again, putting his business face on. "You've got the kind of personality that would do well in the Detective's Bureau. You're one for the details."

"Historic details."

"You'd be surprised how many of our officers have a degree of some sort. I could introduce you."

"No." I decide that everyone will welcome it if I deal with my highly strung sister rather than his weird proposition. "It is a very beautiful ring, Hélène. How did he propose?"

If *he* has any problem with me talking about him as if he weren't in the room, Cédric doesn't show it. Instead, he puts his arm around Hélène again and smiles blissfully while she tells me all about the romantic restaurant dinner Cédric organised.

I'm thankful for the food in my mouth that prevents me from speaking my mind. Everything she describes is like a textbook proposal. Uninspired, flaunting his apparent wealth, making sure every cliché is ticked. He even got the live band to play their song for them. Hélène obviously eats his shit up like chocolate mousse. Ever since she got her first job in finance, she's been obsessed with a bougie lifestyle. Of course, she would love a fancy dinner and an even fancier ring.

I remind myself that I'm not exactly an expert in relationships with all that fretting over a simple library date tomorrow. Sure, Cédric isn't my type by a mile, but he gives Hélène exactly what she craves. He makes her happy, I suppose.

Once Odile and I have cleared the dinner table—Hélène is too good for that now she's an engaged woman—I try to retreat to my room, but Hélène beats me to it. She's leaving Cédric to entertain our parents and pulls me and Odile inside. As soon as she's closed the door, she lets out a jittery sigh. Her eyes are glistening with excitement. "What do you think?"

Odile and I share a glance. Odile obviously has a lot on her mind, but she presses her lips together, leaving it to me to assume my preordained position as the middle child. "We're happy for you."

Hélène's face falls. "Just happy?"

"What do you want us to be? Exalted?"

"We could do a reel replaying the whole thing but with much more screaming and the like," Odile suggests. "It would probably get some decent engagement."

"You should worry more about real life than clicks and likes," Hélène can't help saying. "With all those accounts you're running, it's no wonder your grades have slipped."

And this is where the middle child bows out and takes care of her cute little hedgehog, who's just woken up. While my sisters argue about the financial prospects of social media and Odile's priorities, I get Malou's breakfast ready and lift her out of the cage to give her a cuddle before letting her run around my room.

Hélène plops onto my bed. "There's something important I need to talk to you about."

"You're pregnant as well?" I ask flatly, which sends Odile into an excited gasp. My little sister is living for the drama.

"No." Hélène shudders. "I'm not planning on being pregnant any time soon. I've just started a new job." She clicks her tongue. "No, it's about the wedding. As you know, I will need a witness, and I would love it to be one of you girls, but... well, it can be only one."

"You're gonna pick Alix anyway," Odile says with a groan. She's well aware of the hierarchy.

Hélène sputters, "I-I... yes. If Alix wants to." Her eyes implore me to say yes.

I'm well aware that it's not as serious as it once may have been. Witnessing a wedding is as simple as putting a signature on the wedding certificate. No one is going to come after me if the wedding fails, but technically, the success is what my signature is supposed to guarantee; that to the best of my knowledge, I believe in this union and the two people being joined to uphold their legal obligations.

I really don't want to vouch for Cédric. Not right now, at least.

"Why are you hesitating?" Hélène is visibly deflating in front of me.

"I'm not. I'm... I'm just overwhelmed." And there's not even a ghost to blame this time. "Yes. Yes, of course." In the end, it will be just a signature. It's really not my place to question my sister's relationship. I just can't help it, though. "Are you happy?"

"Am I happy?" Her face softens, and I can see the smile in her eyes before it grazes her lips. "Yes, very. I love Cédric and the life we're building. He's such a hard worker, and yet always finds time to surprise me." She must have picked up on something in my face, because her smile sours. "I know you're not his biggest fan, but he likes you. He always asks me how you... the two of you are doing. He just wants the best for you."

I can't help it; he creeps me out. While Cédric has been in Hélène's life for a little over two years, he still feels like a stranger to me. And why would a stranger be interested in my success? But this time, I manage to keep my lips shut and smile.

"If Alix is going to be your witness," Odile asks while she takes pictures of Malou for her Instagram account, "Does that mean she's also in charge of your bachelorette party?"

"Are you going to have one?" I ask Hélène, panic flooding me. It's not traditional in France, but it has gained traction in the last few decades. Merely the thought of some boozy party spree makes me queasy, though.

Hélène's lids flutter. "Well, I can't exactly plan my own. But I would probably be pleasantly surprised if you... or the two of you organised something." Her gaze flits to Odile. "It's something you could take into hand."

"Leave it to me." Odile seems to grow two inches as she says that. "If Alix were in charge of it, we'd all be doing some spooky cemetery tour."

My sisters know me too well.

Hélène checks on me, worry in her eyes. "You're not still visiting cemeteries, are you? The Panthéon doesn't count." Her question is much more loaded than that. Contrary to Odile, Hélène knows about my talent, though in recent years she's adopted the belief that it's all in my head.

"I'm a history student." It's not much of an answer.

"Alix…"

"If you're going to try to talk me into joining law enforcement, too, I'm going to put Malou into your shoe."

Odile instantly cradles the little hedgehog in her arms, as if I ever risked her health to get back at my sister.

Hélène lowers her gaze and takes a deep breath. "History isn't exactly a degree that gets you a lot of job opportunities."

"I've got a job."

"A side job." But she gives up quickly. "It's your life, your decision. I just think that it…" Her words come out slower and slower. "That it is not the best environment for you. I mean, you could be so much more. As Cédric said, you're smart and detail-oriented." She speeds up again, having found her stride. "You don't have to do law enforcement. I actually have no idea why he would say that. You could do finance or IT."

"Is that Cédric at the door?" I call loudly. "I think I can hear him putting on his shoes."

Hélène shoots me a withering look. "I'm worried about you."

"I've got a degree, I'm enrolled in post-grad studies, and I've got a job. I think I'm doing fine for someone my age." Seriously, what's there to worry about?

"Yeah, if anything, Alix could loosen up a little," Odile chimes in, completely missing the point, but making sure to get a dig in.

My older sister gets up and puts a hand on my cheek. "I'm glad to hear that. If history is your passion, go for it. Just... make sure you pay as much attention to living people as you do to the dead." She goes in for kisses. "Thanks for being my witness."

I stare daggers into her back while she says goodbye to Odile. When she's left the room, I fall onto my bed, letting out a big groan.

Odile is still on the floor with Malou. "She is right, you know. You do tend to get your head stuck in research."

What I tend to do is get wrapped up with ghost business, but I don't see that changing anytime soon. If anything, Hélène's unsolicited pressure only pushes me to dig deeper.

# CHAPTER 6

I'm still in a bad mood the next day when I plonk my bottom down next to Gaby in the lecture hall. It's our Parisian history class where we examine Paris and its role through time, with a huge focus on urban planning. It's also the class that has sent us into the catacombs.

Gaby raises an eyebrow. "What's bothering you today?"

"Family dinner."

"You still have one, or you've already had one?"

I glance at her and slump deeper into my seat. "Hélène came over with Officer Cédric." Officer Cédric is what I call him when I'm alone with Gaby. He has always shown an uncomfortable interest in me, or perhaps his presence just makes me feel like I've done something wrong. Not that crossing cemeteries at night is a criminal offence. "They're engaged now."

"Already? Your sister moves fast. Wow." Gaby doesn't care much about my sister, so her reaction is missing the proper aplomb. She picks up on my mood, though. "Are we against this?"

"What? No." I shake my head. "I mean, yes, but it's not like I have to marry him. Sure, I'm not the biggest fan of... *him*, but that is Hélène's choice and she's happy. He makes her happy," I affirm unnecessarily. "It's really not my place to say something."

"You're her sister. If it's anyone's place, it's yours."

I sigh deeply and straighten myself up again, pulling out my college notebook. "But it isn't anyone's place. Either way, I'd better get used to it. *And* get used to having his unsolicited opinion in my life."

Gaby shoots me a commiserating glance. "Oh no, what did Officer Cédric say this time?"

"That I should join the police force."

Gaby sputters, unable to contain her laughter. "What? Did he smoke some evidence?"

Now I can't hold back my amusement either. "Possibly. Can you imagine?"

"No!" Our laughter garners some looks, but the lecture hasn't started yet, so we're good.

"He's so weird. But Léni is enamoured with him." My mood takes a dip again as I remember how quickly she took over his opinions. "She agrees with him that I'm headed to unemployment with my history degree."

Gaby shrugs. "My parents ask me *all* the time what I'm gonna do afterwards. As if there aren't enough museum or teaching jobs around. It could really be worse."

"Well, you know what she really worries about."

"That history is too close to ghosts?" Only two years ago, Gaby didn't believe in ghosts either. She still can't see them, but that doesn't stop her from wholeheartedly supporting me.

"I don't know why she even cares. It's not like I'm bothering her with them anymore. But it's still the old..." I pitch my voice. "Alix, you need to spend more time with the living and worry less about ghosts."

That garners me another glance from the group of boys seated two rows below us. However, none of them speak up. They know that if they say something Gaby will be at their throats—my friend is protective like that. They just exchange glances, shrug, and continue talking about some soccer game I couldn't care less about.

Meanwhile, our professor, Madame Canet, has arrived, still sipping on a coffee-to-go as she loads her slides. The title word makes my heart sink. *The Catacombs under Paris.* It's accompanied by a well-known picture of piled-up bones and skulls.

"All right, who managed to visit the catacombs in the last week?" Madame Canet asks, casting a glance through the room.

Almost half of our hands go up, including Gaby's and mine. She nods and smiles. "Nice. The rest of you, please get there before the next lecture. It's eye-opening, really. Of those who went, who would like to describe to the rest of us how your visit was?"

"Claustrophobic," Gaby says, then claps her hand over her mouth. "Pardon."

"Yes, Gabrielle. Claustrophobic is a very apt word. Would you care to elaborate?"

With a deep sigh, Gaby accepts her fate. "Well, it's a couple of dirt paths underground in the dark. There's stone on either side of you, and most corridors aren't big enough for two people. And then on the sides, you've got the bones. They're all stacked up on top of each other, making for a rather gruesome sight. Though I found seeing them like that took away the normal creepiness. Like, I think I would have been more scared if I stumbled across an open grave and saw a full skeleton. I know they were real bones and skulls, but still…"

"It dehumanises them," I help out.

"I was going to say it sanitises the whole thing," Gaby says with a pointed look in my direction, then mouths, 'What are you doing?' at me.

Madame Canet's gaze lands on me. "Alix, that's an interesting point you're making." She sounds exhilarated because it's one of those rare occasions that I've opened my mouth in class. "Would you say that the catacombs take away from the whole horror of death?"

"Death isn't horrifying," I say, before catching myself. What am I talking about? Death is *very* horrifying. I just have to ask that woman from yesterday. "What I mean is, I felt very uncomfortable in the catacombs. I know that Paris had and probably still has a problem with the number of bodies buried in the city, but I personally think that the solution of the catacombs is horrendous. Sure, we don't know their names and there's nobody alive who does. They're not important people whose deeds have lasted for centuries, yet I can't help but imagine how I would feel if my bones got separated, mixed, and stacked for tourists to gape at."

"You'd be dead," Théo calls from below. "Or a ghost," he mutters, earning a few chuckles from his friends. And to believe I had a crush on him when he joined the class two years ago.

For some reason, his answer doesn't shock me into silence. "So, you think just because someone dies, they lose their dignity?"

"Alix, please," Gaby whispers.

"If I went to your family's graveyard, pulled out all their bones, stacked them, and turned them into a wall for your room, you'd be happy?"

Théo turns around, takes a deep breath, and then glowers at me. "No, Alix, I wouldn't be. Because I'm not obsessed with dead things like you." There are no chuckles now.

"Then maybe you're in the wrong class," Gaby shoots back at him.

Madame Canet raps her knuckles on the desk. "Guys, please. You're master students, not kindergarteners." She smiles encouragingly at me. "I personally think you're making a valid point. Why do you think the people back then made the decision they did?"

"Probably because it was the most convenient?" I shrug my shoulders, then shake off the uncertainty. "It was a purely economic choice, I assume. The bodies needed to be removed or Paris would've collapsed under the weight of its dead. Nowadays, we would probably burn the remains to make space for new burials, but I assume that wasn't acceptable back then."

Instead of confirming it, Madame Canet's eyes sparkle. "Look it up. I want to see that whole thought process in your work, with proper references."

She turns to her device to bring up the first content slide, which details the life of Charles Axel Guillaumot, the Quarry Inspection Department guy who oversaw the whole reburial process. As she talks about his involvement and how he got himself into the position, I mull over the catacombs as they are today. Théo might not believe in dignity after death—though I'm pretty sure he would object if I were indeed to dig up his relatives' remains—but I've seen what it did with the ghosts. There was nothing dignified about their existence. With all their limbs jumbled up, their sense of self had been deeply disturbed. They didn't even remember who they were, because they were supposed to be already forgotten.

I shudder, cold sweat breaking out on my neck.

"Yes, Alix?" Madame Canet prompts, already having moved on to the next slide.

I never even noticed that I'd raised my hand. Gaby regards me anxiously. "Uhm... Madame Canet, are there any plans for the catacombs?"

"Plans?"

"Well, what's going to happen with them in the future?"

The professor frowns at me. She reaches for her coffee cup and takes a sip. "I'm not sure I'm following you, Alix."

My heart sinks as I already get a grasp on the answer. "I guess they're going to stay like that? A morbid tourist attraction to cash in on?"

"I'm not aware of any future plans. I'm sorry." Madame Canet laughs nervously, but she recovers remarkably quickly. "What would you suggest? Let's pretend this issue is on the table and you're one of the planners making the decisions. What would you do?" She seems incredibly happy to leave her lecture be and embark on this experimental role-play session.

I'm not happy about it. While I feel deeply for the ghosts, I don't have the confidence to make decisions like that. I'd rather help out in the little ways I can. It doesn't help that Gaby hisses, "Let it go."

"Assuming we can agree on this being an undignified way of displaying the remains of actual people," I start slowly, certain people won't agree on that at all, "I would suggest looking into alternative ways of burial." An idea flashes before my mind. "We've got the technology to identify the remains. I'm talking about DNA tests."

"Who the fuck cares?" Théo blurts. "Pardon my language, Madame Canet, but as Alix pointed out already, nobody remembers these people. They are, frankly, just bones."

"They're not *just* bones!"

A sharp jab in my side makes me wince. Gaby glares at me.

Théo rolls his eyes. "Fine, they once belonged to real people. But nobody cares about them anymore. So, why would we pay millions of euros to identify and sort them, only to what? Stack them up in order? Have tens of thousands of skeletons buried nowhere? You're only creating problems, not solving any. Partly because there isn't any problem to begin with."

"Alix?" Madame Canet prompts me to continue the argument.

But I'm sitting there with my lips pressed together, trying my very best to keep the words threatening to spill out. *He can't see the ghosts. He can't see the ghosts,* I repeat endlessly in my mind. If he did, he would see the problem immediately. Everyone would. But I'm the only one who can see them, and that makes me a basket case while the ghosts continue to suffer.

"Théo's right." Something breaks in me as I force the words out. "It is what it is."

There are other solutions, such as a fire burial to release all those disturbed souls, but I've become painfully aware of the ridicule that will faze me if I continue to press the case.

Only Madame Canet seems disappointed with me for throwing in the towel. The rest seems relieved. "Do more research and have a proper think. We can continue the discussion after you've handed in your work."

As she returns to her lecture, Gaby scoots a little closer and wraps her arm around my lower back. In front of me, Théo rolls his eyes once more, then puts it all behind him and pays attention to the slides.

Meanwhile, Gaby whispers, "Just let it go. It is what it is, just like you said. You can't help them all."

"They don't have anyone else to help them," I whisper back.

Her arm around me squeezes a little tighter. "But they already had a life. Why would you ruin yours for them? Let it go, Alix. I mean it."

I stare at her, dumbfounded. "How does this ruin my life?" I mouth.

She lets go of me and scribbles her answer on a piece of paper instead. *I'm scared you'd do something stupid.*

When I raise my eyebrows, she continues. *Like breaking in and sorting the bones. Or setting a fire. Just think about what Officer Cédric would say.*

Annoyed, I grab the notepad from her and scribble my own reply. *I'm not going to do anything!* My pen punches through the paper, causing Gaby to cast me another worried glance.

She very carefully takes the notepad away from me and mulls a whole minute over her answer. A minute I manage to spend actually concentrating on the contents of the lecture. But the answer comes, and it knocks my feet out from under me.

*Good. Don't get mad at me. Perhaps your sister (and Théo) do have a point. You are a little obsessed with ghosts—and yes, they're real, but so are you. I'm worried about you spending too much time trying to make them happy and forgetting about your own needs. When was the last time you cared for anyone alive?*

When I check if she's serious, Gaby gives me a pitiful look. "Sorry."

Unsure whether I'm mad at her or just disappointed, I go through my memories and land on a guy with soft brown hair and an infectious smile. The smile must've jumped onto my face, because Gaby suddenly looks intrigued.

With a feeling of vindication, I write my answer. *Yesterday before class. His name's Gaspar, and I've got a date with him in the library later.* After all, I promised Victor I'd go.

"And you didn't tell me until now?" Gaby asks way too loudly.

"Gabrielle," Madame Canet says sharply. "I hope you're outraged about not having had access to the lecture material before now."

"Of course," Gaby mumbles, sinking into her chair. Once Madame Canet's attention has returned to her lecture, she throws me an intense glare, then scribbles furiously onto our piece of paper.

*TELL ME EVERYTHING!*

Between Gaby squeezing me dry about Gaspar and the anger I'm harbouring on behalf of the catacomb ghosts, I didn't take in much from the lecture. Not that I'm too worried about it. The lectures are interesting, but for me to retain that knowledge, I need to work with the sources myself—be they ghosts or books.

Today's choice of research material is obviously going to be books.

"Promise me you won't let any ghost distract you on your date," Gaby says as she pushes me toward the library.

"I can try." It's not like I make a conscious choice to see ghosts or they're not drawn to me.

Gaby stops me short. She slams her hands onto my shoulders and stares me down. "Try very hard."

I roll my eyes at her. "Way to put the pressure on, Gaby."

Her hands fall off my shoulders and she sighs. "You're right. I'm just so excited for you," she squeals.

"You don't even know him." And neither do I. Not really, at least. I glance at the library with trepidation. How did I manage to get myself talked into this date? That's right, a dead womaniser put notions of love into my head.

"So, which one is it?" Gaby is on her tiptoes, overlooking the long benches in front of us.

Sorbonne's library is a giant study room. The books are stacked on shelves located at the sides, a row of windows above them. Rounded arches separate the shelves, flowing into the curved beams supporting the roof. Along with the rows of parallel benches, it looks like a giant church. The benches are equipped with charming little desk lamps, allowing individual study spaces. The central ridge of the roof is supported by vertical beams rooted in stone blocks decorated with sculptured figures, who watch over the students. It's a place steeped in tradition and history. Students have studied here for eight centuries, including Pierre and Marie Curie more than a hundred years before me.

I try to find Gaspar's floppy mop of hair among the assembled students, but fail to do so. Disappointment hits me. "He's not here." I must be too late. It's almost four o'clock, three hours after Gaspar said he would be waiting here. If he ever was here, he probably decided to leave a long time ago.

"Are you sure? He might be somewhere in the back, or he popped out for a toilet break." Gaby's not ready to give up on my potential relationship.

"He would've been waiting since one. I'm sure he gave up." I should've told him that I wasn't free until four. That's what normal people would do. The only reason I can think of why I didn't tell him smells too much of self-sabotage. "Or something came up, and he forgot." As disappointing as it is, it's probably for the best. This way, I can't ruin the memory with my ghost affliction.

Gaby frowns at me, almost as unhappy as I am. "So, what now?"

"Now, you go to work and I'll get a start on the Paris paper." She should've already left, but was too curious for her own good.

"I don't want to leave you when you need me. I can call in and—"

"Go! I'm okay." I flash her a smile. "You know me. Research makes me happy."

Gaby purses her lips before relenting. "Fine. But if mystery boy turns up, I want a play-by-play this very night."

"I promise." Not that there will be anything to report.

At last, Gaby realises that she's cutting it dangerously close if she wants to be on time, and flees the library. Meanwhile, I stroll through the benches and mark one of the seats near the end of the hall by dropping my backpack away from the chatting groups close to the entrance. Then I make my way towards the history section of the library to select my reading material.

I gather a small stack of books on urban development and mod-ern-era Paris, when my eyes catch on a title. "A City of Light and Darkness — a Guide to the Parisian Catacombs."

Shifting the weight of the stack onto my left arm, I take the book from the shelf and read the back blurb. I tell myself that it is the perfect source for my paper, ignoring the burning curiosity inside of me. It reminds me of the catacombs tour guide I met last night. Just like her, the book describes the catacombs as a giant maze made up of cisterns, ancient ruins, and World War II bunkers. It's a historian's dream. As dangerous—and off-limits—as it is, I kind of want to see it.

Happy with my haul, I return to my seat, where a familiar figure awaits me, sitting on the desk next to my bag. "There she is."

"Gaspar."

Sure enough, Gaspar flashes me a grin, and heat explodes in my tummy as the excitement from the other day rushes back. "I thought you'd left."

Today, he's wearing a light-coloured, open shirt over yet another band shirt. Several dark leather bracelets cover his wrists, between them one bright-pink wristband. I wonder what it granted him access to.

"And miss our date?" he pretends to be offended but can't keep his face straight. "I've been looking forward to it all day."

"Did you?" I have the sudden urge to swipe a lock of my hair behind my ears, but can't because of the books. All day, I've been fretting about the date, almost calling off the whole thing, but now that he's by my side, I can't keep myself from smiling. Gaspar makes it so easy to be around him. "I'm sorry you had to wait. I was stuck in scientific writing."

"Sounds terrific." He slides off the table and plops into the chair next to my spot. "What have you got there?"

I put the books down on the desk and take a seat. "We're currently going through the history of the catacombs."

Gaspar's gaze lingers on my newfound treasure. "You ever been down there?"

"Only the public part." Just like a common tourist. "Have you?"

A dangerous glint enters his eyes, only softened by the wide grin his lips are spreading into. "I have."

"What? How?"

He laughs, and the sound of it makes the heat rise in my tummy. "Don't be so shocked. It's not that hard."

"It's illegal." I lower my voice, worried someone will hear us. "All entries to the catacombs are sealed."

"No, they're not. Some are, but usually, when one door closes, another one opens." When I only give him a blank stare, he leans over and whispers, "The cataphiles open up a new entry."

Inadvertently, I lick my lips. He's almost touching me with his shoulder, causing a flutter in my stomach. "The cataphiles?"

"Friends of the catacombs. It's an illustrious bunch."

I almost tell him about the woman I met yesterday, but remember in time that she's a ghost and I don't want to breach that topic with him just yet. "And you're one of them?"

Gaspar checks the room, then nods. "I don't go in often. Well, I used to, but only for the concerts. They've got some epic raves down there." He leans back again. "You should come along."

"What?" Raves and I don't mix in my head.

"To one of the parties. There's one Friday night. If you're game." He bounces slightly on his chair as he says it, clearly excited about it. "You might've noticed I'm into music."

I glance at the band shirt he's wearing, but don't recognise the name. "Possibly."

"Possibly you noticed or..." he draws the 'or' out and squints as if anxious about what he's about to say, "... possibly you've agreed to a second date Friday night at ten?"

What was I even worried about? Flirting with Gaspar is as easy as breathing. It's as if I've known him for ages. Though it's not what I meant, I answer, "Sure, I want to attend a catacombs rave with you."

A sentence I never would've thought I'd say before now. Odile will lose her mind when she hears I'm willing to go to a party. And such a peculiar one at that.

Gaspar's eyes light up and his grin spreads so wide dimples are forming in his cheeks. "Where have you been all my life? You won't regret this. I promise."

I don't think I could ever regret spending time with him. Underground parties might not be my usual kind of jam, but with

Gaspar, I'm willing to try a few new things. Besides, I'm really curious what the catacombs are like.

# CHAPTER 7

Since I don't have work today, I decide to visit my grandmother on Père Lachaise. As usual, the cemetery is full of people—living and dead. As it's slowly getting dark, the former are starting to leave, which gives me a bit more leeway to discreetly wave at the ghosts I pass. They've all known me since I was a child, first visiting with my father or mother, then later on my own. I wouldn't say I was the only teenager spending their free afternoons at the cemetery, but I definitely would have topped the most-frequent-visitor list if there was such a thing.

My grandmother's grave is in a more secluded part, away from the big attention-seeking mausoleums. She and her best friend Beatrice are sitting on their tombstones, legs crossed and drinking ghost wine, which is nothing but air to me. Their frequent cackles ring out over the cemetery, making my heart sing. It's a morbid thought, but one day, I hope Gaby and I will be the same.

"Alix!" my grandmother calls out, her eyes widening with delight. "Is it that time of the month?" Now that I'm preoccupied with classes and work, I have much less time to visit than back in my teenage days.

"It's almost the end of October," I affirm.

Beatrice's eyes sparkle. "Uuh, we need to get ready for Samhain. Who should we cajole into playing at the party? Chopin was lovely last time, though I suppose we could give Jimmy a shot if he's game. I'm in the mood for some modern music."

Considering that Jim Morrison died over fifty years ago, it's quite a stretch to call his music modern.

I take a seat on the grass, which is still warm from the day's sun, and cross my legs. "How are you?" Subtly, I glance around me to see if I can make out anyone distinctly alive. It's always a tough call on Père Lachaise, but fortunately, most people don't care too much about those who talk to the graves.

My grandmother snorts. "We're as we always are. That's the joy of being dead." She laughs, and Beatrice joins her with a cackle. "The real question is, how are *you*?"

Squirming, I try not to dig too deep into how I'm feeling. "Hélène is getting married."

"Already? In my mind, you kids were only little just yesterday. Is it that guy you don't like? Cédric?" Grandma doesn't need to sound so excited about it.

"Yes, it's Cédric."

Beatrice squeals, equally hungry for details. "Uuh, tell us more."

I swear these two are the worst gossips in town. "There's not much to tell. They got engaged in a really boring way. Well, I suppose, others would find it romantic. And now they're planning the wedding. Léni wants me to be her witness."

"Of course she does. You two were always as thick as thieves." That might have been true when my grandmother was still alive and a couple of years afterwards, but that ship has sailed well and truly.

"I'm not sure I want to be a witness for them. Cédric is just so weird."

"A little rule-stickler, he is." Beatrice nods wisely. "A real brown nose." She spits out. "I'm with you on this one, darling. Nobody wants a boring man."

My grandmother slaps her playfully. "Don't be so mean. He can't be that bad if Hélène has agreed to marry him."

"No, Beatrice is right," I say. "He is that bad. Last time, he suggested I join the police."

It's not exactly comforting how Beatrice and my grandmother burst out laughing. I suppose it is a rather ridiculous prospect, but they could be a bit more sensitive. Then again, that's like asking the sky to be a bit more red.

To avert the unwanted attention, I broach another topic. "Question. A ghost asked me to look into this. Do you know someone by the name of Julien Cadeaux?"

The two of them share a long glance before my grandmother tells me, "His grave is about five minutes from here. Why?"

"Well, I've got his…" I still don't know what the relationship between Julien and Penelopé truly is. "His lover, Penelopé Feroulet, was wondering why she wasn't buried with him. Apparently, she'd bought the plot next to him."

Another shared glance. This is going to get juicy.

Beatrice tugs on her neck scarf and puts on a great show of innocence. "Oh, I mean, this is just a rumour, of course, but Julien was the one who bought the plots… but he didn't put it in his will."

"Why would he not do that? Was it an oversight?"

"Well…" Beatrice clicks her tongue.

My grandmother puts it more bluntly, "She was just the affair, you know. He never planned to be buried next to her." She rolls her eyes. "He was so annoyed that she kept showing up at his grave, always tearful. Quite the little martyr. His words, not mine."

I sigh. Romance is officially dead… at least in ghost Paris. "So, when he moved on, he *actually* moved on?"

"Oh, *he's* moved on." Beatrice giggles. "Believe me, Alix. That man doesn't even let a body go cold."

My stomach turns at the thought of it. "He'll probably be glad he's rid of her now."

"Maybe." My grandmother shrugs. "It wouldn't surprise me if he starts missing her after all. Men can be like that."

"Yeah, but not all," I protest almost instantly.

Both stare at me with sudden intensity. "Is there a particular man who's not like that?" my grandmother asks innocently.

I can feel my face heat up. "I wasn't... Yes." I lower my head, preparing myself for the inevitable drilling that will happen now.

Beatrice squeals again. "Who is it?"

"What's his name?" my grandmother asks.

"Is he good-looking?"

"Smart?"

"Rule-breaker or rule-stickler?"

The heat intensifies. "I suppose he's more of a rule-breaker. He's invited me to a rave down in the catacombs. We're going Friday night."

Another salve of questions is fired at me. My gossip grandmothers—Beatrice is my adopted ghost grandma—can't wait to devour this delicious piece of information.

I gladly indulge them with all the juicy details this time, because talking about Gaspar makes me happy as well. Friday can't come soon enough.

# CHAPTER 8

**M**y nerves are absolutely fried by Friday night. I can't believe I'm going to trespass in the catacombs. I can't believe I'm going on a date, either. But apparently, the real confounding thing is that I'm attending a party of my own free will.

"You never go to parties," Odile points out while she's hanging out in my room while Gaby gets me ready for the party. "Much less a rave."

"There's always a first time," I mumble before Gaby flicks my chin up to do my eyes.

Contrary to my little sister, my best friend is excited. "Exactly," she exclaims. "I love this for you. It's high time you developed an adventurous streak." Odile snorts, but Gaby ignores her. "Maybe once you get a taste of it, we can go clubbing. You could be my wing woman. Help me with the girls."

"Maybe." I try my best not to blink too much. My heart is racing at the sheer insanity of tonight's adventure. This isn't me. I'm not the kind of girl who sneaks out to wild parties. Though, in this case, it's not the sneaking out that's the issue, but sneaking in. "I wish you would come."

"And crash your date?" Gaby asks, outraged. "I would never. Besides, I don't think you'd have much fun with me in that kind of environment."

Gaby is claustrophobic, so a night in the catacombs might be exciting on paper for her, but not so much in real life.

"I could come," Odile offers with glistening eyes.

"Don't you dare!" Gaby points the mascara at her before applying it to my lashes. "She's already got company. Gaspar will take good care of our girl."

I refrain from pointing out that she doesn't know him well enough to make such a claim, because the mere mention of his name makes my stomach dance before it even gets to the rave. "He'll be there, right?"

"Of course he will be. It was his idea." Gaby takes a seat in my chair. "From everything you've told me, he's extremely eager to spend more time with you. He'll be there."

Odile sighs loudly. "It's like a disease. One sister gets engaged and suddenly the other is falling into the arms of a stranger. Don't make me go to two weddings in a year."

"Wedding?" I ask, drawing in a sharp gasp. "I've just met the guy."

"And you never meet anyone. This might be your only chance."

"Odile, go take some selfies or do your homework," Gaby snaps at her. She rolls her eyes at me when Odile finally leaves us alone. "With sisters like yours, you don't need enemies."

I smile at her, grateful for my third 'sister'. "What should I wear?"

Gaby jumps up, excitement flooding her again. She pulls out a couple of outfits from my cupboard and throws them on the bed. "Don't worry. I've got some ideas."

In the end, I'm wearing a casual get-up: a pair of jeans, a long tunic under a half-length leather jacket, and a beige neck scarf, the kind Beatrice wears. My long, wavy brown hair falls over one shoulder. While Gaby spent a lot of time on my make-up, it only enhances my natural features, almost as if I wasn't wearing any at all.

Gaspar asked me to meet him on Rue de Sèvres, but when I get there, the street is entirely empty. I try to listen for the telltale bass of a dance club, but the road looks like a residential area, not a club in sight.

Of course. The party isn't up here.

I glance at my feet, imagining the hidden world beneath the asphalt. How are we supposed to get down there? Surely, the entry isn't in any of the apartments on either side of the street.

Nervously, I recheck the address. But before I can fret too much, Gaspar arrives. He's wearing a hoodie, both hands hidden in the front pocket, head down. He looks up as he comes closer and takes out one hand to wave at me. "You're early."

"On time." More or less.

He leans in to exchange kisses, and my breath catches in my throat. While I've exchanged kisses with people countless times, this is the first time Gaspar's skin touches mine. His cheek is rough after a day's growth of stubble, but my stomach still somersaults.

Unaware of my sudden reaction to him, Gaspar glances around. "Did they open the entrance yet?"

"Entrance?" I cast around, unsure as to what he means. "Are we in the right spot?"

Gaspar laughs, and the sound of it is like warm chocolate. "You'll see. I hope you don't mind getting a bit dirty." He takes a moment to take in my get-up, his eyes sparkling under the streetlight. "You look great."

Heat rises in my cheeks. "Back at you."

While he's hardly wearing formal wear, the street style suits him. His hair is fashionably tousled, some of it falling into his eyes, forcing him to flick his head frequently. He grins at me, and I realise that for all I care, he could wear a burlap sack. As long as he smiles at me, he's the cutest boy I've ever met.

A scraping sound behind me startles us. I glance over my shoulder and gasp.

In the middle of the street, the round cover of a manhole moves. Someone is opening it from the other side. "Gaspar," I whisper.

He threads an arm around my middle. "It's go time."

"Wait. Are we..." My head goes back and forth between him and the opening manhole. Suddenly, my stomach plummets and my knees are made of gelatin. "Are we climbing down there?"

Gaspar seems amused. "What did you expect?" He takes my hand and pulls me towards the opening. "Come on."

Meanwhile, a man has popped up from it, casting his gaze through the street as he catches his breath. "Is that all?"

"I believe so." If someone else was supposed to come, I wouldn't know.

The guy shrugs and ducks down again. "Very well. Make sure no one's watching when you climb down. Be careful on the steps. They're a bit slippery today, and one feels a bit brittle, so take it slow. I'll go back and close up after you later."

We arrive at the manhole, and I can make out a metal ladder on the side. The guy is already halfway down the shaft. Gaspar throws a glance over his shoulder, then urges me forward. "You go first."

"I'm not sure I..." The dark hole is daunting, like a gaping mouth.

Gaspar turns to me, his chest nearly pressing against mine. He locks eyes with me, his ever-present smile tugging at his lips. "Do you trust me?"

I want to say that I don't know him well enough to trust him. One look into his eyes, though, makes me *want* to say yes. Odile might have exaggerated a little, but she might have been on to something. This exhilarating, heart-thumping thing I've got going with Gaspar is too beautiful to risk. I haven't felt like this in a long time. If ever.

"I do," I whisper.

"Then let's go." His eyes sparkle, and some of his excitement laps onto me and brings back the feeling in my knees.

With newfound determination, I lower myself onto the edge of the manhole and reach for the first surprisingly thin metal rung. Our guide was right. They feel a bit slick. Under Gaspar's guidance, I swing my legs in and place them below me, only putting weight on the rung when I'm sure it'll carry me. Then I slowly climb into the darkness.

I've never quite understood Gaby's fear of tight spaces, but this gives me a pretty good idea of what it feels like. While the manhole is wide enough for a much bigger person to climb down comfortably, it *is* a vertical shaft that goes down for ages. And since Gaspar follows me, blocking out the little light that falls in from the streetlights, I'm doing it based entirely on my sense of touch.

Swallowing heavily, I concentrate on each individual rung as I descend into the sewage system, anticipating the two unstable ones the guide mentioned. Soon, the smell hits my nose, distracting me from the oppressive feel of the stone walls around me.

There! The next rung gives when I put my foot on it. Panic seizes my throat, and I jerk my foot up again. I force myself to take a couple of deep breaths, then reassess the situation and go for the next one down.

Warm light flickers below me, making it easier to orient myself in the darkness. Then my feet hit solid ground. I've arrived.

"Welcome to the underground," our guide greets us with a toothy grin and a flickering torch. He goes back up as promised, practically flying up and down the ladder. This certainly isn't his first time on the rodeo.

Once the guide has returned, he waves us along. "Come on then. We won't have long to go."

We follow him along the slippery ledge, and I try not to think about how the catacombs are supposed to be this giant maze. Right now, it's just a sewer, running straight under the street. It's surprisingly warm down here, about fifteen degrees or a little less, but everything is muffled. There's no air draft, no sound from the city, and not much to see outside the narrow cone of light the torch provides.

Our guide spouts off a couple of cool facts I've heard before and probably told tourists about at one point. Instead, I focus all my senses on my surroundings, taking in this surreal underground world. There's no light apart from the one we brought, and yet the walls are full of tags. Loads of people have been down here, perhaps even attending a party like I am.

After a turn, we meet up with a larger group who must've been picked up from a different entrance. Our guide leaves us with the new group to go back for stragglers. My pulse calms a little, now that there's the constant buzz of hushed conversation and excitement, as well as several lights. For a while, we continue following the sewer, then we turn into another tunnel. We turn two more times before our guide opens up a door and leads us down a set of stairs.

Gaspar slips his hand into mine and whispers to me. "I know this one. The rave's going to be in the Room of Cubes." We're the last ones to enter.

As it turns out, the Room of Cubes is an old World War II bunker, with five-metre high walls, that are partially painted with a cubic pattern, like from one of those illusion books. You can't tell whether the cubes point outwards or inwards. The number of stroboscopic lights flashing in rhythm with the beat doesn't help with that. Not that I care enough for it.

Music surrounds me. The beat is thrown against the walls and repeated tenfold in my stomach. In my free time, I listen to soundtracks and musicals, and a mix of rock and pop music, not these aggressive rhythms that command your body to move. Normally,

I wouldn't last a full song of electronic music, too dependent on beautiful lyrics and well-composed melodies, but in this environment, it gets my blood boiling and my pulse rushing.

The room is packed with people, their bodies pressing against each other as they hop and bop, completely lost in the music. With the flashing, multi-coloured lights in an otherwise darkened room, I can't make out any faces, which makes all of that extremely overwhelming.

At least, until I look into the only face I need to see. Gaspar laughs at me, the sound swallowed by the beat. He's enjoying this without a single reservation.

Someone bumps into me from behind, and suddenly my body is pressed against Gaspar's as the other person pushes past me to enter the fold. Gaspar's hands find mine, and he pulls me with him toward the side of the room. There, he leans into me, his breath caressing my cheeks. "Shall we stay here?"

The embarrassment about my reluctance to throw myself into the crowd is swept away by the warm feeling of gratitude that washes over me as I realise he's putting my needs above his. Without ever taking his gaze off my face, Gaspar moves our arms above our heads and starts dancing with me.

I completely tune out the big, undulating mass of people in our vicinity and concentrate on the beautiful man in front of me. His dancing and the music completely loosen me. The bass is reverberating in my stomach, and even though repetitive chords fill my ears, it's like I can hear my pulse in line with the beat.

"How do you like it?" Gaspar shouts into my ears. He has to repeat the question before I understand him.

"It's great!" Maybe later, I will elaborate, but at the moment, I'm all out of words.

Gaspar doesn't need anything else. He grins from ear to ear and swirls me around, so my back presses against his chest. I could stay in this position all night.

The DJ finishes his set three songs later and hands over to the next. She's got amazing style with turquoise hair in two messy buns and a bold matching lipstick. When she asks how we're doing, we all scream incoherently. I spare a thought for Odile, who will never believe I did that. And had fun!

A little later, Gaspar leans in again to ask me whether I want a drink.

"Yes!" I haven't even noticed, but I'm absolutely parched. All that dancing has taken its toll.

Gaspar guides me to the other side of the room, deftly sidestepping the completely out-of-control attendees. Hidden from our previous spot is a bar. It's not a permanent fixture, only a table full of bottles. I'm pleased to see that most of them are water. It's only when I empty half the bottle in one big gulp, I notice how dehydrated I was becoming.

I have no idea whether it's midnight yet or long past, but fortunately, I'm not Cinderella who needs to be back home before the dance finishes. Gaspar and I continue to dance with each other, laughing wildly as the DJ spins her records.

After an hour or two more, my feet are getting tired, and I stumble more than I dance. Exhausted, I cast a glance through the room. I'm just about to ask Gaspar whether he knows where we can rest—and maybe spend some time talking instead—when I notice a couple of dark figures hurrying down the stairs, flashlights in hand. They shout something, but the music swallows their words.

Noticing my distraction, Gaspar follows my line of sight. His eyes widen, and he grabs my hand. "Come with me!"

"What's happening?" I shout as he pulls me along the wall, past the people to our side.

We're still on our way through the room when screams arise. The music cuts off, and the DJ shouts into her microphone. "Cataflics." She abandons her set and flees from the platform.

The cataflics. In other words, it's the police.

My heart is suddenly hammering against my chest. When I thought about this evening, I was nervous about a lot of things. Running from the police was not one of them.

Gaspar keeps pulling me along, narrowly evading the crowd spilling to the sides now. I can't see where he's going. There's only the cube-painted wall in front of us. We're right behind the DJ, who extends her hand towards one of the cubes, grabs hold of something I can't see, and rips open a door that was completely hidden in the illusion.

We and a good portion of the people around us squeeze in after her.

Darkness swallows us, and I feel my way by Gaspar's pull and the people pushing me from behind. A good number of them get out their phones, their lights exposing patches of the path. It's a great idea, and I fumble for my phone. I get the light to work just as we burst through another door, leading out to a raised platform.

The mass behind me nearly pushes me over the edge, if not for the railing. But before I can even catch my breath after noticing the empty hole below me, Gaspar pulls me to the side, and we run down a set of stairs.

Behind us, the police are shouting, imploring us to stop being stupid and halt. My legs nearly give way in fear. Running into the catacombs seems like a really bad idea, but people are pushing me from behind, while Gaspar keeps pulling me along in a hurried but unpanicked manner. He seems to know exactly where he's going.

We no longer follow the DJ, and I notice that the crowd has dispersed in different directions. A few follow us, but with every turn and twist, there are fewer people around us.

The corridors have changed. They're no longer the smooth concrete of World War II bunkers. Instead, they're made from brick now, and by the looks of it, old and crumbly bricks, quite similar to the part of the catacombs open to the public. Just without the bones.

A light dances behind us, and I press myself against Gaspar, afraid the police are after the two of us. He takes another turn, ducking into a narrow corridor that forces us to move sideways. With my body squeezed between two stone walls, a new fear enters my mind. What if Gaspar only looks like he knows what he's doing, and we're getting lost deeper and deeper in the catacombs?

But then, we break free from our confinement, stumbling into a much wider, upward-sloping corridor, firm and packed, almost like a proper street. The light of my smartphone washes over rough-hewn walls that seem much more stable than the crumbly section we just left behind. I keep the light in front of me as I follow Gaspar.

Just then, I hear a cough to my side. I whirl around, and my flashlight illuminates a figure under a blue street sign. To my surprise, I know her. It's the woman who came to visit me at the Panthéon. The ghost seems as surprised to see me as I am to see her. Then I remember that she was a catacomb tour guide and knows her way around here.

"What is it?" Gaspar tugs at me, causing the beam of light to drop to the ground. "We're almost out."

When I raise my phone again, the ghost is gone. I guess, with Gaspar choosing his path without a second of doubt, we don't need her help. I nod at Gaspar, and we continue our rapid ascent.

A few minutes later, our surroundings are starting to grey, and I pick up a slight draft. Mad laughter bubbles up inside me when I realise that we're going to make it out of here with no police on our heels.

The exit is blocked by a gate, but someone has cut the bars on one side and created an opening just wide enough to squeeze through. Gaspar helps me, and then we're out, emerging into what looks like a former quarry exit that's now overgrown with weeds. We climb up the steep side, using our hands and feet, and finally collapse on top of the bank, laughing.

Above us, the stars are shining. We must be in one of the outer suburbs or just outside the city for us to see them. I inhale in the night air, adrenaline still rushing through my veins. We're alive. We're here. We're free.

Gaspar still clasps my hand. He turns to the side and simply gazes at my face as if he's drinking me in. "That was..." Whatever it was, he doesn't have enough breath to say it.

There's a moment where we simply gaze into each other's eyes, listening to the accelerated pulse of our living bodies. And then, as if on cue, we both lean in. His hand is suddenly on the back of my head, while our lips meet in one breath-stealing kiss.

My lungs ache, but I don't want to break the kiss that's searing my lips. Gaspar opens his mouth, and my tongue slips beyond his teeth, tingling when it touches his. The pressure on my head increases as he pulls me even closer. Our mouths become one, the playful swirling of our tongues my single point of focus as all else falls away.

That first kiss is rushed, fuelled by adrenaline and passion, but then our bodies relax. We separate to take a breath, gasping loudly. When we come together again, it's much more gentle. Gaspar kisses the corners of my mouth, taking time to explore the shape of my lips, while I run my hand through his hair, delighted that it's really as soft as it looks.

"You're one heck of a woman," Gaspar whispers. "Sorry that your first time down there was cut short by those damn cataflics."

I try not to think too much about the fact that I've just run from the police. Then again, all we did was dance and have a good time. Not exactly the hard-boiled crime my brain is imagining. "Thanks for taking me." I kiss him again before whispering into his mouth. "That was amazing."

For a few minutes, we leave all the words behind and sink into the kiss, exploring each other's mouths as we do so. His hands stroke down my back, but they never stray too far, instead coming to rest in the small of my back. Meanwhile, my fingers stay entangled in his hair as I take my breaths directly from his skin.

It's not until the dampness of the grass seeps into our clothes that we break off. Gaspar gets up to his feet and pulls me up, once more taking in my sight.

"Let's get you back home." He puts his arm around my shoulders and starts towards the city. From the looks of it, we are quite a bit away, though there are buildings rising not too far from us. I can see why they call it the city of lights from here. Thousands of sparks in the distance, illuminating the dark shapes. The Eiffel Tower rises from the sea of lights like a beacon calling us home.

I lean into Gaspar and smile up at him, then kiss him on his cheek. "Thanks for taking me on this adventure."

"Anytime, Alix. Anytime."

# CHAPTER 9

I wake around lunchtime to the incessant ringing of my phone. From the ringtone, I can tell it's Gaby. Groggily, I search for the phone, cursing when I realise the charger hasn't been plugged in completely. I've only got about eighteen percent left. Hardly enough to tell Gaby everything she wants to know.

"You woke me," I complain into the phone anyway.

On the other side, Gaby giggles. "Sorry, darling. That sounds like you had a long night, though."

"It was amazing." If I close my eyes, I can still feel Gaspar's lips on mine. "Listen. I'd love to tell you all about it, but my phone's almost dead. Meet at *Noisette*?"

"Absolutely. See you in an hour."

I put the phone back on the charger, this time checking that it's actually charging, and close my eyes again. Last night was so much fun. Sure, the police chase was kind of the opposite, but even that was exhilarating and only added to the mad rush of feelings that led to my first kiss in three years. I still can't believe how quickly everything went, but I guess love can strike fast sometimes.

After a few more minutes of daydreaming, I can't contain myself any longer and reach for the phone again. Gaspar gave me his number last night, and it's time to check whether he thinks as much of me as I do of him. I agonise over the first message and settle on a non-committal, "Hey, sleepyhead. Are you already up?"

Apparently not, as I wait several minutes for a reply. I get out of my bed and check on Malou. The little hedgehog is deep in her burrow, sleeping. Did she miss me last night? I leave her in peace and get dressed, frequently checking my phone without any luck. Like Malou, Gaspar has turned in for the day.

From the sounds of it, or rather the lack of them, my family has fled the coop, which saves me from an intense grilling by Odile. I forgo breakfast—or lunch—and follow their example so I'll get to the café in time, pocketing my phone despite its low battery. I don't want to miss the moment he wakes up so I can tease him about the beautiful weather he's missing out on.

The sun has warmed up Paris despite the late October date. By the time I lock my bike near *Café Noisette,* I shrug out of my jacket and enjoy the sunshine on my bare arms. Still no message, though.

Gaby is already waiting, having managed to grab a table on the plaza. She greets me excitedly, her eyes big with curiosity as she runs her gaze across my face. "Tell me all of it," she says before we even sit down.

I start with the strange descent into the catacombs and the Room of Cubes, while I wait for my coffee and a brioche with lettuce, ham, and Camembert. "There were so many people, everyone just dancing as if there was no tomorrow." For her benefit, I give her a detailed report on how I danced with Gaspar and how his body felt against mine. It brings up all the warm fuzzy feelings I woke up with this morning.

When I get to the police crashing the party, Gaby gasps. "Damn it, girl. You really don't do boring, do you?"

I laugh. "Guess not! Though, to be honest, I was scared out of my mind. Especially when Gaspar and I were all alone in the catacombs. I thought we were lost. But apparently, he knows his way around. I have no idea how he did it, but he got us out of there." I only realise now that Gaspar seems to have a deeper knowledge of the catacombs than he previously let on. If I understood the complicated politics down there correctly, he's probably one of the cataphiles exploring the catacombs at his leisure.

My heart races at the thought of him taking me deeper into the maze, fulfilling all my historian dreams.

"Good on him." Gaby looks earnest. "If he would've got my girl lost, he'd be in big trouble." But her serious mood doesn't hold long. She leans forward, grinning wildly. "So, the two of you got out. And then?"

"Then we kissed." I burst into giggles, while Gaby squeals, garnering a few looks from the other patrons.

I can't stop laughing. Last night was amazing, the feeling only strengthens as I tell Gaby about that part in all the glorious detail. "His hair is so soft," I sigh. "I could just sink into it."

"Sink into his lips. That should be more fun." Gaby wiggles her eyebrows.

"Fine." I almost throw my last bite at her but decide to devour it instead. "Thanks for pushing me to go."

Gaby grins proudly. "That's what friends are for." She reaches over the table to squeeze my hands. "I'm so happy for you."

My excitement endures the entire day. At work, my tours are filled with romantic details of my favourite ghosts. It certainly spices things up a little, and perhaps it's not quite what people expect from a Panthéon tour, but I couldn't care less, because my head is filled with thoughts of Gaspar.

At the end of the day, I'm even humming as I pick up the trash. The ghosts around me seem amused, and Victor shoots me a knowing look. I'm just about to call it a day when I suddenly find myself face to face with the catacomb tour guide. "You."

She obviously doesn't share my excitement, her intense gaze scrutinising my face. "I've had another thought about this. And I'd like to hire you."

"Hire me? I don't... What can I do for you?" I ask with a sigh. You can't really call it hiring somebody if you're unable to pay the person. And ghosts usually don't have money. "Maybe start by telling me your name?"

She stares at me, unblinking. Then her shoulders relax. "Pardon me. My name is Emily Durant. I'm still new to this," she raises her arms and lets them fall again, "existence. I don't know the rules. But another... ghost, I suppose, told me about you. That if I needed something done—something I can no longer do by myself—you'd be able to help."

"Not with everything, but I'll try my best. What is it you need doing?"

"I need you to retrieve something for me." Emily licks her lips before she continues. "I... I lost it on my last tour."

It takes me a moment to realise what she's hinting at. "You mean in the catacombs?"

"Yes." Her eyes meet mine again, and it's as if she wants to convey something just with her look. "It's quite deep in, past the Banga and the Crossroad of the Dead."

My lids flutter. "Excuse me?"

Emily smiles faintly. "We've always been quite creative when it comes to naming things in the below. You were at the party the cataflics crashed, right? That's pretty accessible. Where you'll have to go, only a few people know the way."

My heart is pounding against my ribs. Now it's me who licks her lips, finding the courage to ask, "How am I supposed to find my way, then?"

"You'll find a cataphile who knows. I saw you with one last night."

"You know Gaspar?"

Emily shrugs. "Not closely, but I've seen the kid around. He knows enough to get you in."

I try not to listen to the increasingly loud voice in my head that tells me this is pure madness. There's no harm in gathering information, right? "Why can't *you* guide me?"

"Alix." Suddenly, Victor is at my side, shooting the woman a withering glare. "This is not a favour you should take on."

"Who are you?" Emily asks brusquely.

For a second, Victor stares at her in disbelief. "You don't know who I am? Does the name Hugo ring a bell? Victor Hugo?"

Emily squints. "Were you a musician?"

The lack of respect and knowledge renders Victor speechless, so I cut in. "He's a famous writer. The author of 'Les Misérables' and 'The Hunchback of Notre Dame'. And many more," I quickly add.

"Oh, that one. Sorry, I've never been a big reader." And with that, Emily dismisses one of the great figures of France. "Anyway, I need you to go to Ossa Arida. That's deep down in the catacombs. I can guide you after the Crossroad of the Dead to... where I think I lost it."

"What did you lose?" Normally, ghosts aren't that stingy with details, especially not if they're sending me into a place of questionable safety.

Emily hesitates yet again. "Something very personal to me." Her mouth stays open until her eyes suddenly light up. "A medallion. My mother gave it to me, and I want my daughter to have it."

My heart goes out to her. Judging by her age, unless she had her as a teenage mother, her daughter is still young. To have lost your mother so early in life is heartbreaking. Having at least something—and something so personal—to remember her by almost makes me want to agree to the job instantly.

And I would've, if Victor hadn't recovered from the shock and squeezed in between us. "We will consider it. If you don't hear from us, it means no."

Emily tries to peer past his massive body, her eyes filled with desperation. "Please! There's no one else I can ask. It's important."

"I know," I assure her, despite Victor's interference. But his interruption has given my brain some time to catch up. Doing this favour comes at a huge risk to myself. This won't be a quick excursion into the catacombs to a place with plenty of people. Rather, I would have to walk deep into the maze to a place called

Ossa Arida. *Dry bones.* A place that can't be found on any map, because mapping the catacombs is forbidden.

But Emily's right. The ghosts have no one besides me. It's my weak spot, the one argument I find impossible to ignore. "Listen, I'll have a chat with Gaspar. And if we can come up with a proper plan, I'll do it."

"Thank you." The relief pouring out of the deceased tour guide is staggering. "Thank you so, so much."

"You should go now," Victor announces. His eyes find one of the many generals buried in the Panthéon, drawing his attention.

Emily understands the threat and quickly retreats towards the doors. "I'll meet you in Ossa Arida."

The minute she's gone, I realise I've never found out why she couldn't guide me to Ossa Arida in the first place. I turn to Victor, displeased with his unusually brusque demeanour. "Since when are you my manager?"

The portly ghost sighs heavily. "I'm a friend, Alix. And believe me, the catacombs are no place for you."

"Why not?"

"Because they're dangerous!" he says, a little forcefully. "You don't know this woman."

I roll my eyes. There are many ghosts I didn't know while they were alive. "She's dead."

"If you're trying to say she can't hurt you because of that, don't. You're a ghost whisperer. Any ghost or human can hurt you. And there are plenty of both sorts where you think about going."

A cold shiver runs down my spine, cooling my fire. "What are you saying? The catacombs aren't full of people. Surely, there's no more than a handful of cataphiles."

Victor snorts. "A handful of the worst kind of people."

"Uhm, may I remind you that Gaspar took me down there for our date? He's a cataphile."

"That's right. You should probably forget about him."

His prompt answer knocks the wind out of my sails. "What?"

Victor completely disregards my outrage as he elaborates. "Well, this man is obviously a danger to you. When we talked about him, you said he was a sociologist, not a catacomb crawler. That's a big difference. An important difference."

I'm too confounded by his unexpected vehemence to counter his words with proper arguments. "You encouraged me to give him a chance."

"As I said, I didn't know any better. Now that he has exposed himself as a cataphile, I'm advising you to stay away from him." Victor might call it advice, but his insistence makes it clear that I should heed his words. "He already got you in trouble dragging you down there."

Victor might not think much of it, but I had an incredible night I would argue was worth every bit of trouble. "Nothing happened."

"Because you got lucky." Victor sighs once more and the tone of his voice mellows. "Alix, there's a reason these people hide in the shadows. Perhaps your lover is only a thrill-seeking rule breaker, but there are a lot of people down there who use the inaccessibility and darkness of the catacombs for their nefarious business. Think of Thénadier. Take another favour. One that doesn't put you in mortal danger."

I keep my lips pressed shut. He's certainly managed to dampen my desire to take on Emily's favour, but I can't help it. The snapshot I got of the catacombs last night only served to whet my appetite. I want to see more of it, investigate the different kind of corridors, and learn all about the rooms. There's a city below my feet, waiting to be explored. I don't want that one date to be my last venture into there.

Torn between caution and curiosity, I'm unable to tell Victor what he wants to hear. "I'll think about it." It's all I can offer him for now.

I grab my things from the staff room and lock up behind me. As I walk down the stairs of the Panthéon, I eagerly reach for my phone, expecting a million messages in the meantime. But the only thing that greets me is Instagram notifications for Malou's profile

Not a single text from Gaspar.

# CHAPTER 10

Twenty-four hours and close to a dozen messages later, I'm feeling utterly miserable. Gaspar has gone completely cold on me, and my heart doesn't know what to make of it. It aches for him with an intensity I've never experienced before. The only thing keeping me alive is the fact that my phone shows he hasn't actually read any of my texts. I tell myself that there is a good reason for it, but the thread of hope is becoming thin.

To distract myself and potentially cry with her later, I invite Gaby for a sleepover. Originally, my pretext was to work on our class papers, but we only manage half an hour of that between Gaby ranting about her mother—who's forcing her to join her on a family trip next week—and playing with Malou. By the time the sun has set, we are halfway through my meeting with Emily.

While Gaby has never questioned my ghost-seeing ability—an encounter with a ghost cheetah and the uncovering of a crime while helping a dead-showgirl-turned-war-hero will do that to you—she isn't the biggest fan of my ghost adventures. "I'm sorry, but I'll have to side with Victor on this one. The rave was one thing, but crawling into the seedy underbelly of Paris? That's a bad idea."

"How do you know it's—"

The door to my room opens, and Odile strolls in, eyes glued to her phone. "Hey, did you get Hélène's message? She wants us to shop for bridesmaid dresses next week."

"I thought she didn't want bridesmaids?"

Odile looks up from her phone, but only to roll her eyes at me. "She doesn't. *But* she wants us to wear something nice, regardless. Something matching. You know, for the pictures." Her voice is fraught with tension.

"Of course." Leave it to my sister to extend her need for perfection to what we'll be planning on wearing. Eager to get Odile out of my room again, I agree to it. "Sure. Hope Hélène's buying."

"Oh, yes. I don't think Maman will agree to give me next month's allowance. Oh, wait, she already did, but two months ahead would truly be too much."

"What happened to—" I stop myself in time, remembering that I wanted her out of my room. "If it's for the wedding, she might give us some."

Odile's face lights up. "I'll ask her. Be right back."

Although she leaves my room, the door remains wide open. Gaby gets up and closes it firmly behind her. "So, as I was saying, this one's just too dangerous. There's a reason it's illegal to enter the catacombs. It's a bunch of unmapped, confusing, crumbling paths." She shudders. "Please promise me you won't go there."

"If I do, it will only be with a guide like Gaspar." Mentioning him makes me choke up a little, but I clear my throat and continue. "And we'll stick to the safe paths. I mean, Emily obviously managed to go there and lose something, so the place I need to go can't be crumbling."

"How did she die again?" Gaby asks in a fake cheerful voice.

Before I can answer, Odile dashes back into the room, knocking the door into Gaby's elbow. "She said—oh, sorry, Gaby. Why are you standing behind the door? Did you want to leave?"

"No," Gaby says with the patience of an angel. "What did your mother say, Odi?"

If Odile has detected the underlying tension in Gaby's voice, she doesn't show it. Instead, she grins wildly. "She's going to give us a hundred euros each!" She jumps up and claps excitedly. "I'll check out styles." And she's off again.

Gaby gives the door a determined little push. "Gosh, that girl can be annoying. Doesn't she have like a million friends she can discuss these things with?"

"Don't be mean. She's just excited."

"And you're not?" Gaby walks over to sit down again, scooping Malou up on the way. She gives the little hedgehog a finger to hold on to, which is so adorable I could die.

103

It takes me a minute to remember the question. "I'm not super excited, no. But that's okay, it isn't my wedding."

"Will we ever see your wedding? To Gaspar perhaps?"

I moan when his name slips over her lips. Then I grab my phone and check it for what is surely the millionth time today. "He's not texting me back. He hasn't even looked at my messages."

"That's good." Gaby lets go of Malou and scoots closer to me. "I mean, it sucks, but if he hasn't seen them yet, it means his phone is probably dead or something. He's not ignoring you."

"If you say so." I don't know a single person our age who leaves their phone off for forty-eight hours. He's ghosting me and not in the good way. "Or he's had his adventure and is off to invite the next girl to a catacombs party. I'd better find out how else I can find my way in."

Gaby's eyes widen, and she turns pale. "No, absolutely not. You're not setting a foot into there without a guide. Or with a guide. Alix, this is—"

"I've had the cutest idea!" Odile announces as she barges back into my room. She casts around until she finds Malou, who is trying to climb over a pile of history books I had stacked in the corner, before picking her up and presenting me with my own hedgehog. "How about I make a matching bridesmaid dress for Malou? She *has* to attend the wedding."

"She'll probably be asleep through the whole thing," I remind her of Malou's nocturnal lifestyle.

It doesn't quash her optimism even a little bit. "She'll still look cute. And she'll be awake for the reception. It's going to be a proper wedding, Alix, not just some courthouse ceremony at lunchtime."

A courthouse ceremony sounds divine to me, but Odile is right. Knowing Hélène, she would want to make it a big, fancy affair. She'll probably book some country house and make us all stay there for a weekend. "Fine, make Malou another outfit." I have an entire drawer of them.

"She'll look so cute," Odile promises and leaves again, my hedgehog in tow.

"Door!" Gaby shouts.

Odile's head reappears. "Sorry," she says, as if we offended her. "I'll leave you two alone."

"Hedgehog," Gaby says, unimpressed by my sister's catty response.

Odile sets Malou back on the floor. Then she looks at Gaby, her eyes narrowing. "You should probably get a dress, too." The door bangs shut, giving Malou a fright.

Gaby stares at the door in disbelief. "What was that?"

"That was my sister's way of saying you belong to the family and will likely be invited." I pull Malou onto my lap and give her some belly rubs to alleviate the shock. "Don't take it personally, sweetie. Odi wasn't mad at you."

Gaby rolls her eyes before continuing where she left off. "You know, instead of planning dangerous expeditions into the cavern system below our feet, you should concentrate on your sister's wedding. Either to stop this madness or find the fun in it. Otherwise, they'll tear you apart before you can come up with a plan for the bachelorette party."

"It's easy for you to say that. You can't see or hear the ghosts. But there's a woman who died and—"

"Exactly!" Gaby's eyes turn pleading as she reaches for me. "She's dead, Alix." Her fingers stroke my knee. "Nothing you can do will bring her back. You've got your own life to live. You don't need to hold onto theirs."

# CHAPTER 11

The last few days have been torture. Gaspar keeps ignoring my texts. In a moment of desperation, I even call him, though I end the call before it can ring more than once. He doesn't react to that either. Him going cold turkey on our fledgling relationship leaves me reeling in a way I would never have expected. When Théo distanced himself, I couldn't have cared less, but now even the ghosts can't distract me from my unrequited yearning.

And yearning I do. I sit in the library every day and keep expecting to catch a glimpse of him on campus. I even start buying my coffees from *Chambelland,* but I never catch him on shift. It's always his coworker, Marie, who looks sad all the time. Too sad for me to work up the courage and ask her about Gaspar. I keep wondering whether she and Gaspar had a fling once, and he pulled the same shit on her, hence her icing him out the morning we both entered.

When the yearning is slowly replaced by resignation, I throw myself into further research. So far, I've kept my promise to Gaby and Victor. It isn't too hard, since Emily never calls on me again. Perhaps she's moved on as well. Ghosts aren't exactly known for their attention span. But the curiosity Gaspar sparked in me—*damn him!*—makes it impossible for me to let go. I read all there is about the catacombs, first of all the book that I found in the library.

As often happens when I make my way through history books, I completely lose myself in it. The catacombs are utterly fascinating. They aren't just a hidden layer under the earth, but their own city. It's as if the city has been built on top of itself again and again. Somewhere in the deep are the ruins of Lutetia, the Roman settlement. Then there are medieval structures and the old cemeteries which prompted the decision to move the bones. The same tunnels have been used for cooling, water storage, and sewage before being repurposed into war bunkers. The city below has swallowed it all, and I shudder, thinking of how it will swallow us one day as well.

The relationship between cataflics and cataphiles is an interesting one as well, though the chapter is a bit lacking in specifics. It probably costs a lot of tax money to keep up the fight against the cataphiles, but if they didn't, tourist ventures would likely seize the opportunity and endanger people. There's already some secret underground tourism going on. I haven't dared to look too much into it, but I feel, with my research abilities, I could totally find the right person to contact.

I would much rather it was Gaspar, though.

Ugh, I hate that he still has a hold on my heart.

It's been a week since our magical night and even more magical kiss, but he's been ignoring me ever since, and I need to move on. A part of me resents Victor a little for telling me to put myself out there, only to turn around and order me to break off the relationship, as if none of that involved any feelings. The joke's on him, however, since I never got to break things off with Gaspar.

I really need to stop thinking of him.

"There you are."

I very nearly jump out of my seat. The voice I've been wanting to hear for an entire week is suddenly in my ear.

Slowly, I turn to the side. Sure enough, as if my thoughts finally summoned him, Gaspar is standing in the aisle. His eyes light up and there's the grin I yearned so much to see.

The butterflies rush back into my tummy with a force that sends me reeling. He was gone. He ghosted me for a week. He left me. But all that doesn't matter to my stupid hormones. They just listen to one tune: he's back.

It's not fair that any man should have a smile that can shut off brain circuits so completely.

I clear my throat, cautioning myself about getting too excited. "Uhm, yes. I'm here. As I was yesterday. And the day before. And the day before that." I'm proud that I got that out. He can't just expect to waltz into my life as if he didn't leave me hanging dry.

The smile falters, and I can think again. Good. I'll need to keep my wits about to protect my heart from him.

"About that..." Gaspar comes closer and slides into the chair next to me, eyes fixed on the edge of the table. "I had a bit of a family emergency." He swallows.

And just like that, all my resistance crumbles. "I'm sorry to hear that." I reach out with my hand but catch myself before I can touch his shoulder. "I've texted you like a million times." As bad as it sounds, a simple text should've been possible, shouldn't it?

Gaspar looks up, surprised. "You did?"

He pulls out his phone and taps the screen. It stays ominously black. Gaspar swallows again, then presses the on the power button for what seems like an eternity. The phone remains dead.

The breath catches in my throat when I see his face twist in pain. His eyes look so tormented. "Alix, I'm so sorry. I didn't mean to ignore your texts. Stupid thing just won't work." Disgusted, he throws his phone across the table.

His shoulders deflate. "You must think I'm the worst, but I'm just—"

"It's okay." I throw my arms around him and hold him tight. Whatever emergency has occurred in his family is obviously really bad. Staying mad because he ignored my needy text assault is just petty. I stroke his back. "Do you want to talk about it?"

Gaspar hesitates for a moment, then shakes his head. "I'd rather not."

That's okay, I tell myself. Despite our wonderful night together, we hardly know each other. What he needs right now is compassion and perhaps a distraction. "If you want to know, my texts were really embarrassing. Like the first few were... full-on swooning."

He chuckles softly, then raises his head. His face softens, and he blows a kiss to my cheek. "If it helps, I was swooning pretty hard, too. You might be my dream girl."

The butterflies slam into my tummy again. It truly does help a lot to know I'm not the only one in love with that night. "Really?"

"Really." The smile creeps back, and it's as if the sun dawns on my skin, leaving behind a trail of goosebumps.

"We could do it again?" I ask shyly. Please let him say yes.

"What?" The spark is back in his eyes. "This?"

Gaspar bridges the distance between us and softly kisses my lips, as if he, too, is too shy to fully commit.

I welcome him in, feeling my cheeks burn with the most delicious warmth. Oh, how I've missed the sensation of his lips and tongue on mine. But that wasn't what I meant.

"I was talking about visiting the catacombs," I whisper between kisses. Yes, I know I promised Victor and Gaby not to go, but Gaspar needs cheering up and the catacombs are his second home. That much was clear from how easily he found his way to the outside world.

Gaspar breaks off the kiss and laughs. "You've got the cataphile bug!"

My cheeks redden. "Is that so obvious?"

"A little." He grins wildly now. "I knew you would fall for them the minute you set foot in them. It was the same for me. They're just so cool. So, do you want me to investigate the next rave?"

I glance at my research material. "Uhm... actually, I found the tunnels we ran through afterwards much more interesting." Obviously, I can't tell him about Emily Durant. Just like Gaspar won't talk about his family emergency, I'm not ready to disclose the fact that I can talk to ghosts. Not yet. "Perhaps we can explore a little bit."

"Sure. Did you have anything specific in mind? Like what bits you're most interested in? I haven't been everywhere, but that shouldn't stop us."

I love how there's a "we" now. Doing favours for ghosts is usually solitary work, unless I can rope Gaby in to help me. But Gaby wants me to focus on my life and thinks this favour isn't worth the risk, plus she's claustrophobic, so the catacombs are a nope for her.

An idea sparks and I point to the book, as if that's where all my information comes from. "I read about a place called Ossa Arida. Dry bones." I shrug with a coy laugh. "I told you, I'm into that."

"And I love that!" His enthusiasm fades, though, and he frowns. "I've never heard of that place."

There goes Emily's idea of letting Gaspar lead us.

He looks around nervously, and his frown deepens. "Let's go to the back. There's someone watching us."

While he gets up, I glance over my shoulder and my eyes land on Théo, who sits three rows behind me, wearing a scowl on his face. It's a bit creepy. He hasn't shown any kind of romantic interest in me for two years, so why would he care about me meeting up with a boy now?

Well, he can scowl as much as he wants. He's been such an ass to me, I haven't an ounce of interest left in him.

Instead, I grab my bag and the books and follow Gaspar to the back of the library. We get comfy behind a shelf, out of sight and out of earshot.

"Okay," Gaspar says with a serious face. "I've never heard of Ossa Arida. If it exists—"

"It does." I hope he doesn't ask me how I know, but Emily was quite confident in the location of her missing medallion. "It's beyond the Banga."

Surprised, Gaspar stares at me. "You know about the Banga?"

"I love research." Sure, I have no idea what the Banga is and why it's so important, but that's what Emily said. None of the names were in the book I read, though.

His face softens again. "Told you: dream girl."

Playfully slapping his shoulder, I giggle. "Stop that. So, how do we find Ossa Arida?"

"You're really keen on that one, aren't you?" He takes a moment to think, clicking his tongue. "In that case, we'll need to find a map."

"A map? I thought those didn't exist. The book said it was illegal to map the catacombs."

Gaspar gives me a rueful smile. "Everything about the catacombs is illegal. The rule with the map is no myth. They want to discourage people from exploring them on their own. But maps exist. The council has some for the upper parts. As for the whole thing..." He checks around the corner of the shelf and lowers his voice to a whisper. "I've heard Nexus created one."

"Nexus?"

"It's a mystery organisation that rules the catacombs. Well, maybe not rules, but they basically live down there. Obviously, they're cataphiles, but no one knows who's part of it and who isn't."

I'm intrigued. You couldn't make this up if you tried. "How do we get in touch with them?"

"I might know someone who can help." Gaspar toys with a thread on his hoodie.

The suspense is killing me. "Who?"

"Le Chevalier d'Os."

*The Knight of Bones.*

I shudder. My mouth feels dry, but the curiosity is killing me. "That's a weird name."

Gaspar snorts. "You don't say. I've never met him, but I've heard stories. Apparently, he knows the catacombs like no other. I bet my ass that he's a part of Nexus. He might not confess to that, but it doesn't hurt to ask him how we could get our hands on a map."

"Does that mean you know where to find him?"

To my big relief, Gaspar nods. "Yes, and you'll like that as much as your dry bones. Le Chevalier d'Os holds court at the Crossroad of the Dead."

While he grins, my thoughts wander to my conversation with Emily. The Crossroad of the Dead was the other place she mentioned, the one she'd said I would have to go through.

"So, are we going?"

I realise I've left Gaspar hanging. Adrenaline rushes through me at the thought of embarking on this adventure with him. I lean over and kiss him excitedly. Oh yes, we're definitely going!

# CHAPTER 12

B efore Gaspar and I can embark on our adventure, I meet my sisters in Le Marais to look at dresses together. I'm not a huge dress person, preferring fitted pants and a loose-flowing shirt, but for an event like this, dresses are a must.

"Do you even know when you're going to have the wedding?" I ask as I look through the monochrome collection of light-blue dresses in an upscale boutique. Some of the shiny ones put me off the colour completely.

Hélène reaches in and pulls out a dress with a blocked-out bustier and a sheer skirt from below the breasts to the ankle. "Next spring. Cédric has pulled a few strings, so we'll get to do it in a beautiful chalet by the sea down near Marseilles. You'll love it. Some writer used to live there. I can't remember who, but the chalet has a tiny exhibition."

Not even the prospect of soaking up some local history can excite me for this event. "If it's by the sea, I'm not wearing that." While the sheer fabric has a layer beneath that blocks the view, the fabric is so thin the wind will blow it around my ears.

"You're probably right. You need something stiffer." Hélène sighs. "It would make for pretty pictures, though."

"Only in movies."

Hélène frowns at me. "What's with all this negativity? Did something happen?" She checks whether the coast is clear, then leans in to whisper, "Are the ghosts troubling you?"

Her framing annoys me. Very few ghosts have ever troubled me. "Nope, all good in ghostland." Sure, there's a ghost who wants me to descend into the catacombs, and Victor Hugo explicitly warned me about going, but that's a dilemma, not trouble. A dilemma I've already solved. I will do it. Gaspar and I will be in and out in no time.

"Then can you at least pretend to be happy for me?"

It's on the tip of my tongue to tell her about my reservations about Cédric. Everything is moving so fast. They moved in together only half a year ago, and within another few months, they'll already be married. What's the rush?

But before I can get into a fight with Hélène, Odile shouts out to her from a couple of rows further down. "You have to see this, Léni."

My moment of courage—or self-serving whine—has passed. I contemplate following Hélène, but the idea of feigning the proper excitement turns me off. Instead, I walk along the rack, my gaze drifting past all the dresses, until entirely different garments catch my eye.

Stepping out of the sea of dresses into the outdoor wear is like leaving a stuffed house to take a walk in the park. The clothes here are practical and sturdy, no embarrassing wardrobe malfunction-in-waiting. I gravitate towards a khaki fitted jacket with elbow pads. Depending on the condition of the tunnels, it might come in handy to wear something I don't have to worry about getting dirty.

I lift the jacket off its hook and find a mirror to try it on. The inside of it is lined, and despite its sturdy outside, it's soft and warm. Plus, it has several pockets. And not that I'm vain or anything, but it looks good on me. Stylish.

The frowning face of my older sister appears over my shoulder. "You're certainly not wearing *that* to my wedding."

"It could get cold by the sea," I quip. When Hélène's face falls, I giggle. "Relax. I'm not buying this for your wedding."

"But you are going to buy it?" The frown deepens. "Are you planning to go on a hike?"

"Something like it." Telling her about the catacombs is completely out of the question. I've already got Victor and Gaby breathing down my neck. I don't need Hélène to pull out her big sister card.

"Is Gaspar taking you?" Odile butts in, a dress over her arm. For Hélène's benefit, she explains, "He's getting her to try out all kinds of things. She even went to a party last week."

If I didn't know Odile had never even met Gaspar, I'd say she adored him already. "It's not such a big deal."

Hélène looks at me as if I told her I was planning to skip her wedding. "You're seeing someone?"

"It's all very new," I hasten to say. Judging by her tone, she seems hurt I didn't tell her. And until now I haven't even thought about it. We used to be close, but that all changed when she got too old for my ghost "shenanigans". "I would've told you, eventually."

She crosses her arms in front of her chest. "I see." For a moment, she looks like she's got a whole lot more to say, but instead, she straightens her shoulders and raises her chin a little. Hélène is too mature for petty fights. "Will he be your plus one for the wedding?"

Behind her, Odile makes a face before ducking towards the changing rooms with her dress.

"We're not at that stage yet." Didn't she hear me when I told her how new it all was? We haven't even shared our deepest secrets yet. How am I supposed to know whether he'll be around next year?

The thought of having to tell him about the ghosts eventually makes my heart ache. I'm not ready for him to turn his back on me and look at me like Théo does nowadays.

Hélène's still doing her best to sound unaffected. "Well, make sure you tell me before I finalise the guest list."

She makes it sound as if the wedding is next week. A discomforting thought. I'd rather tell Gaspar about seeing ghosts and risk his withdrawal than welcome Officer Cédric into our family so soon.

But if this wedding is going to happen, I would love for Gaspar to be by my side. When I try to imagine my future, I come up with all kinds of things I want to do with him. I don't think I've ever fallen this fast and deep with someone.

Once we're done with the catacombs, I will gather my courage and open myself up to him. I know I've got to do it if I really want us to have a future.

# CHAPTER 13

When I meet Gaspar the next day, I'm wearing my new jacket and matching pants. I've also brought Malou with me. The little hedgehog has a carrier bag she enjoys very much. Malou might not be able to see ghosts, but she can sniff them out. Ever since I found out about it, she's become my little companion. With her at my side, fulfilling the favours isn't quite as lonely.

Not that I'm going to be lonely today. Gaspar awaits me at the gate we exited after the rave. He's wearing his usual hoodie, a small backpack, and thigh-high waders that fill me with trepidation. My pants are sturdy, but they're not waterproof. If Gaspar thinks I'm not dressed for the occasion, though, he doesn't let on, instead greeting me first with kisses on the cheek and then a proper one.

Just as I'm about to sling my arms around his neck and truly sink into the kiss, he breaks it off and scrunches up his nose. "Wait, did I just feel something moving?"

I lean back, laughing. "Oh, yeah. Gaspar meet Malou." I reach into the bag to pull Malou out. "Malou meet…" I search his face for the answer, but all of his attention has been diverted to the hedgehog in my hand as he lets out a delightful gasp. "My boyfriend." His reaction to Malou cements my definition of our relationship.

"She's adorable!" Yep, he's totally fallen in love with Malou on sight.

Malou raises her snout, searching for the new smell. I show Gaspar how much she enjoys belly rubs, and delight when Malou holds onto my finger and yawns.

"She's tired," I explain, as if that wasn't clear. "Time to hit the bed, Mademoiselle." Gently, I lower her back into her bag.

"So, you're a hedgehog girl?" he asks, his eyes glistening.

I curtsy. "One hundred percent. Nocturnal and too curious for my own good."

Gaspar laughs. "I guess that makes me a hedgehog boy, too, then." I'm positively swooning. He offers me his hand. "Let's go to where it's night all the time."

In the daylight, the area has lost all of its magic, just another desolate area in desperate need of repair, overgrown with grass and weeds. That lack of repair serves us well as we climb through the hole in the gate. Even this close to the outside world, the oppressive shadow of the catacombs envelops us instantly. Ahead of us lies nothing but darkness. And in this darkness, secrets are waiting to be discovered.

"Do you ever worry about the cataflics closing up an entry while you're down here?" I ask Gaspar as the hole of light behind us gets smaller and smaller.

He laughs. "Not really, no. Because there's at least half a dozen other exits I know of." But then he stops, takes my hand, and pulls me to him. His lips graze mine. "You wanted this, remember?"

I swallow heavily. The weight of my decision bears down on me. I haven't told anyone where I'm going, just left a message on my desk for peace of mind. My mother knows that I'll be late, potentially staying over at Gaspar's, but she doesn't know that *Gaspar's* is the catacombs. If it takes us longer than expected, there will be no way to send a message. I hadn't had a cell phone signal since we entered, which also means I can't call for help. Until we resurface, we're on our own. But as dreadful as the thought might be, I won't let my irrational fears deter me from my mission.

"I do." I whisper into his mouth. "It's just..."

"Thrilling?" I can feel his mouth stretching into a smile and kiss him.

Scary would've worked too, but I get what he means when he says thrilling. This is a risky adventure, but the fear doesn't scare me off. It excites me. "Something like that."

He kisses me back, and it's as if his adrenaline gets injected into my veins. My nerves are on fire. "Let's go then."

We descend further, quickly leaving the light behind us and heading deeper into darkness. This time I've brought the head-

123

lamp my father once bought for camping and then never used again. It may not be pretty, but it lets me cast around while keeping my hands free, one of which is needed to hold Gaspar's. I have a couple of batteries in my backpack and a smaller flashlight in case it fails. I might be too curious for my own good, but I'm not stupid. This is riskier than a secret party underground.

When we were fleeing the catacombs, I didn't pay a lot of attention to my surroundings. So far, the walls around us are unspectacular, just an access tunnel for the ancient quarry cut into the limestone. My fingers sweep across the stone and come away slightly damp and white. Some kind of moss is growing in patches, its surface grainy, but soft under my fingertips.

We come across the street sign under which Emily stood the other night, which surprisingly isn't completely random but indicates the street we just came from. "Is that normal?"

"The sign?" Gaspar asks to confirm. "Yeah. You'll find signs like that all across the catacombs. We don't actually want people to get lost, you know." He laughs softly. "People also light candles and note down directions. So, if you know your way around Paris, you should be fine, even if we get separated." He instantly squeezes my fingers tighter. "Which won't happen. But for safety reasons, just remember rule number one. Don't panic."

"Huh." Because that worked so well for me last time. I suppose the situation was enhanced by the sudden appearance of the police and the turmoil around me. "I'll try."

"You're already doing so much better than I did the first time."

I'm not sure if that's true, but I choose to believe it. Right now, despite barely being able to see two or three metres ahead, the catacombs don't scare me. Instead, they fascinate me.

As we go deeper, Gaspar tells me about the community that has formed down here. "It's basically like a commune. We even have our own honour code."

"Which is?" How bad can the cataphiles be if they have an honour code?

"Practically, it's all about respecting the place. You carry out what you take in, and you respect the past. Like you can create something carefully—there's so much amazing art down here—but you can't destroy anything that's been there before." In the dim light of my headlamp, his grin has a ghost-like quality. "You'll love it. And then there's the code of conduct, you know. Share your resources, no money exchange, just bartering or gifting. Help when necessary. And don't sniff around other people's business. Don't ask where people entered or where they're going to exit. Unless you need their help to leave, of course."

That last one doesn't quite fit with the others, but I suppose it makes sense since we're all trespassing here for some reason or another.

"Come. I'll show you one of my favourite places." Gaspar tugs at my hand and draws me to the side, where he finds a crevice with frightening accuracy. It's a tunnel that leads to a small staircase so tight we have to shift our bodies slightly as we descend it. From there, the path takes a couple of twists and turns that make me wish I was taking some sort of note of where we're going. Not that I'm planning to get separated from Gaspar, but it's a discomforting experience to put your life into someone else's hands so completely. Despite his delicious kisses and infectious smile, he's still pretty much a stranger.

We arrive at an actual door, which hangs slightly skewed on its hinges. Gaspar makes a flourished blow, letting me discover this secret for myself. The door barely moves when I try the handle. I push my shoulder into it to correct the angle before giving it a well-measured shove. It opens to an eerie blue light.

He helps me squeeze through the gap onto a high walkway over-looking an enormous cavern built from multiple slender arches. Daylight falls in from the side. From our vantage point, I can't see if it's coming from windows or holes in the wall. What I can see is water. Beautiful, pristine water, so clear, I can see the pipes and hidden walkways underneath. Small bridges connect a couple of platforms on the side.

"What is this place?" My voice travels through the cavern, echo-ing hollowly.

"Le réservoir de Montsouris. It's tap water, sourced from the River Vanne."

I shudder at the enormity of it all. Like many Parisians, I've never thought twice about where our tap water actually comes from.

It's drinkable, that's all I needed to know. Until now. Now I'm mesmerised by the unearthly blue filling the cavern below us. "It's beautiful."

Gaspar smiles at me. I can see the pride in his eyes. Guiding me here probably gives him a kick all of its own. "Sometimes, I go down here just for that view. It's a great reading spot, away from all that noise upstairs."

I can imagine it well. Paris is a lot. All noise and colour, while this place is serene. I wish we could stay here for a while, but Gaspar urges me to return to the path.

"It's still quite a way until we reach the Crossroad."

The next time we find water underground, it's the opposite of the reservoir. The ground beneath our feet is slowly becoming muddy. I don't see the water until I step right into it. Surprised, I jerk back, my beam of light reflected on the black water. There are no hidden windows down here.

My heart jumps into my throat as I cast around the low-hanging cavern. Contrary to the precise architecture of the reservoir, this place is uneven and rough. And filled with water from side to side. "What is this?" Surely, we're not planning to wade through the water.

Then again, Gaspar might be wearing those thigh-high waders for a reason. He looks at me curiously. "I thought you knew about the Banga."

"*This* is the Banga?" Internally, I curse Emily for leaving out any specifics.

Sure. Go through the Banga, find the Crossroad of the Dead, and keep going until you stumble into Ossa Arida. It sounds so easy when you're not underground in a dark maze with a million dead ends.

"Didn't they say anything about that in your clever books?" Gaspar sounds amused. "This is where we separate the true cataphiles from the casual catacomb crawlers. It's a water lock that you have to pass through to reach the deeper parts of the catacombs." He regards my pants, then shrugs. "You and Malou can go piggyback on me."

"Are you sure?" I'm a grown woman after all, not a small child.

Gaspar gets low, offering me his back. "Yeah, I know where the ridges are. Just keep your head down. The ceiling gets quite low."

This is the last point of return. I can still call the adventure off and return to the outside world. A cup of hot chocolate and a book would be a much better alternative, but I've always said some things need to be experienced, and there's no book that will tell me what lies past the Banga.

Since he seems so confident about it, I decide to trust Gaspar. I make sure that Malou is secure and hop on his back, where I readjust the bag so there's no chance of Malou falling into the water. He catches me under my thighs while I wrap my arms around his chest.

"Ready?" Gaspar asks as he pushes through his legs until he can set his feet.

"I think so." I don't want him to carry me any longer than he has to.

Slowly, we wade into the murky water. If there is a ridge, I don't notice it. Gaspar feels around with his feet before each step, choosing his path deliberately. My beam of light dives into the water and is reflected on the surface and the ceiling. I try to keep my head still, so Gaspar can see where he needs to go, but I can't help myself.

"What's that?" I ask when my light bounces off a set of half-submerged iron bars.

"Cells," Gaspar huffs.

I don't ask him for details since he sounds out of breath, instead making a mental note to check where the Banga lies in relation to the surface city. The Place de la Bastille, perhaps. That would fit.

The water gets deeper and deeper until my shoes touch the surface. The silence around us is nerve-wracking. I can hear each drop that falls from the ceiling, invisible to me and my narrow beam of light.

Gaspar was right; the ceiling is quite low. As my feet start to dip into the water, I press myself against his back, nuzzling my head into his shoulder to escape the stone above me.

"Your breath tickles," he says between huffs.

"Sorry."

"No. I love it." Gaspar stops and searches with his feet. As we actually rise a bit above the water, I'm forced to flatten myself even more. "We're almost there."

I don't make it across with dry feet, but the rest of me, and most importantly, Malou, stays dry when we wade out the Banga on the other side. Gaspar sets me back on my feet and straightens his back as he catches his breath. I feel sorry for having forced him to carry me.

He notices my worried gaze and grins. "Congratulations. Now you're a proper catacomb crawler."

"You did all the crawling. Are you okay?"

"Never been better." His voice sounds a bit hollow, though. "No, seriously. Shit like this makes me feel alive. Not shit," he hurries to say when a dismayed moan escapes my lips. "I meant, I live for this. You're not a burden. Quite the opposite."

"Please don't pretend I'm light as a feather. I don't need flattery." I'm in perfectly normal shape, but almost any kind of body is heavy to carry for an extended amount of time.

Gaspar chuckles. "You're not going to trick me into saying you're heavy." Then he steps closer and puts his head exactly where

I had mine during our crossing, his hot breath stroking my neck. "I loved carrying you."

I don't understand how he can, but I'm not one to argue when his breath does these amazing things to me. His lips are so close to my skin I can feel the goosebumps travelling down my neck to my fingertips. The darkness makes it even more delicious. My light beam bounces off a flooded dungeon, useless to my eyes.

Gently, Gaspar breathes his kiss into the nape of my neck. "I. Loved. Every. Single. Second. Of. It." Each word is punctuated with another kiss up the muscles of my neck and down the length of my cheek until he kisses the corner of my mouth.

Once again, I wrap my arms around him, intercepting his mouth before it can slip away. Time stands still down here in the darkness, where all I can hear is our breath, the blood rushing through my ear, and the soft smacking sounds of our tongues engaging.

Eventually, I gasp for air. Only then I notice that my feet have become cold. "If you kiss me like that afterwards, I'll let you carry me anytime."

Gaspar laughs. "Deal." He takes my hand again. "Let's go. The Crossroad of the Dead isn't too far from here. We'll probably meet some people."

When we finally reach the crossroad, we're not meeting *some* people. We're meeting hundreds.

All of them dead.

# CHAPTER 14

The Crossroad of the Dead is a junction of two slender high-ways in the fractured street grid that comprises the largest part of the catacombs. They widen at the crossing itself, creating something of a square. Several candles have been lit on shelves around the crossing, allowing me to take it all in. The ceiling above us is at least six metres high, and I can see some sort of balcony in one corner created by a former road that has been severed. A centuries'-old cave-in, I assume.

I'm not sure who named the place, but it fits like a glove, because under no circumstances are all of these people alive. If it's not the sheer number of moving bodies that gives it away, it's their attire. I catch a glimpse of a group of three who wear similar clothes to Gaspar, all equipped with waders, huddled in a corner, but most of the rest are dressed entirely inappropriately. I see a woman in a sheer garment with sharp edges who could walk the runway of the Paris fashion show anytime. She's gallivanting with a soldier from what looks like World War I, laughing at something he says. There are old-fashioned waistcoats and voluminous dresses that would've made Marie Antoinette proud, but also many wearing simpler clothes, workers and vagabonds. And if all that wasn't proof enough, I see children. Happy, unsupervised children down here in the catacombs.

I'm a ghost whisperer, but I've never encountered this many ghosts in one place. Not even Père Lachaise is this full.

Six million remains. That's how many bodies they moved to prevent Paris from collapsing into itself. And I think I found out where they buried those that aren't displayed in the tourist section. Now that I'm looking for it, I can see the bones in the walls around us.

But that doesn't make sense. The ghosts in the other place were pulled back into existence after centuries of rest due to people "remembering" them suddenly. Who remembers these? Everything I thought I knew about ghosts has turned upside down. I'm bursting with the need to explore these new findings and readjust my perception.

Next to me, Gaspar swallows heavily, his eyes fixed ahead and his cheek twitching slightly. The sight of him reminds me that I cannot, under any circumstances, let on what I'm seeing. My heart yearns to converse with these ghosts to find out where they come from and, perhaps most importantly, what they're doing down here. But I can't do any of it. I need to ignore them and try my best not to bump into anything that Gaspar can't see.

Not that I have to worry much about him noticing anything. Gaspar moves around the Crossroad of the Dead as if *he's* the one who's never seen the place before. His gaze sways from side to side, crawls up the walls, and gets stuck looking over his shoulder as he stumbles after me.

"What is it?" I whisper softly, clutching his hand tightly.

Gaspar takes in a shuddering breath. His head snaps back to me. A smile springs to his lips, but for the first time it feels forced. He's unable to keep his eyes trained on me. "What do you think?"

Uh, difficult question. I think the place is magnificent. It's like I'm back in upside Paris, but now all the commuters and tourists have been replaced by the dead of centuries. But this isn't the right moment to tell him about the ghosts. Not when he looks this close to freaking out already. "Uhm, it's much... bigger than I thought. Do you know why they call it the Crossroad of the Dead?" I'm mostly asking to snap him out of his funk.

"Bones." He swallows again. "I think it's because of all the bones. Do you see the bones?"

Do I see the bones? I see the whole fucking bodies. "Yes. Yes, I see them. Now, where's that guy you wanted me to meet?" The three cataphiles in the corner aren't the only ones. I spot a couple more living among the crowd, all blind to the ghosts around them, but there are so many bodies moving around, I will never find anyone.

"Who?" Gaspar stares at me, dumbfounded.

"Are you all right?"

He finally manages to shake off the stupor and focus on me. "Yes, yes, I'm all right. Sorry. The chevalier. Let's see if he's there."

The grip around my hand is tight and a little sweaty. It doesn't necessarily fill me with confidence, but I keep my mouth shut and concentrate on moving naturally behind him. We pass the other catacomb crawlers who raise their heads curiously but don't reply to Gaspar's mumbled greeting.

My steps echo in the darkness, because in reality, only very few people are here. The hollow sound and the surreal sights leave a dusty taste in my mouth. I'm not sure I'm ready to meet anyone, and I wish we were back at the Banga, saying no when Gaspar asked me whether I wanted to cross.

But before I can come to a decision about what to do with my sudden doubts, Gaspar leads me to a set of makeshift stairs hidden behind an alcove. It leads up to the broken street on top of the crossroads. Or rather, the dark corridor behind it.

"He should be up there." Gaspar nods towards the stairs. "You go up. I'll make sure no one disturbs you."

"You're not coming with me?" My heart jumps up my throat at the thought of facing this ominous knight of bones by myself.

Gaspar smiles faintly. If that's supposed to be encouraging, it does nothing for me. "You'll be okay with him." He glances around, clearly nervous about something. "Shout if you need me."

I want to say I need him now, but it's time to put my big girl pants on and do what I came here for. This is my mission, after all.

Just as below, the street is filled with ghosts, though these aren't moving. Instead, it looks like I've stepped into a ghost tavern. Dead people are sitting together on benches that some catacomb crawler must've carried up here. From the chatter, I catch snippets of philosophical discussions, current politics—as in current when they died—family woes, and more. They don't actually drink anything, but they definitely enjoy each other's company.

What strikes me most is that many of them are mismatched. The groups gathered don't consist of one era. An aristocrat from the court of Louis XV with a distinct scar on his neck sits together with a flapper girl and a World War II soldier.

Before I have time to find out what these three have to talk about, my eyes are drawn to the only light beside mine. The lamp sits on a bench close to where the former street has broken off. The man and two women who are sitting around it all wear modern clothes. I startle when I notice the man staring at me.

He's between thirty and forty years old with coiffed dark hair and a trimmed beard that makes his face even more angular than it already is. Even sitting, I can see that he's tall and wiry. An athlete, perhaps. Under the low light conditions, I can't make out much more, but the two women suddenly get up, store something in a backpack and leave without giving me so much as a glance. The guy stays seated. Waiting.

"Bonjour!" I call out, my voice pitching. "Are you le Chevalier d'Os?" He doesn't look like a knight, but who am I to argue with someone adopting "bones" as a title?

His unflinching stare makes me swallow heavily. "I..." I force myself to take another step.

A muscle twitches on his cheek as I approach him and he folds his hands under his chin, leaning slightly forward. "That depends on who's asking."

"I'm Alix." I don't feel like giving this unnerving man my full name.

His features relax just a little bit and I can make out the hint of a smile. Languidly, like a cat, he gets up. "Enchantée." I was right, he is tall. I'm not a small woman, but he's still more than a head taller. "And to what do I owe this pleasure?"

I notice that he still hasn't confirmed his identity. It bothers me until I remember what Gaspar told me about the etiquette rules. Don't stick your nose into other people's business. "I was told to come to you if I needed a map."

"Mapping the catacombs is illegal." His voice barely changes at all when he's talking. He would make a great poker player.

"Being in the catacombs is illegal." The words just lend themselves to be spoken.

It works. The corners of his mouth twitch upwards. "True. So, tell me, Alix." As he speaks, he approaches, slowly circling around me. "What brings a pretty girl like you down to such a dirty place?"

I stiffen, his words crawling under my skin. Instinct makes me want to turn around and ask Gaspar if we can meet with somebody else. But there is no one else. Le Chevalier d'Os is the only one who deals with maps. Emily is no help and I don't know where else to turn. I only know it's too early to give up.

Thinking of Emily appears to have summoned her. She suddenly stands on the edge of the road, her eyes wide.

"Alix?"

The chevalier's voice behind me startles me. I realise that I've been staring into the distance instead of answering his question. "Uhm." I turn to him, using the movement to gather myself. "I'm a history student. And there's a place that I would like to check out. For research purposes." It's an excuse that has come in handy before.

"How wonderful." The chevalier is full-on smiling now, shedding his wariness like a coat of fur. "Well, I don't want to get in the way of important research. I might be able to procure a map for you, but it'll cost you."

"No!" Emily snaps.

Her sudden interruption startles me. Flinching from thin air, I must look absolutely crazy to the chevalier now. "Sorry, I thought I heard something," I fib.

"Don't barter with him," Emily continues regardless. "You shouldn't even talk to him. You don't want to get involved in his schemes."

Her sudden worry makes my legs shake. My stomach feels as if it's filled with stones, like the wolf's in *Le Petit Chaperon Rouge*. No matter how much I wet my lips, my mouth stays dry. "I didn't bring any money."

"We don't barter in money down here."

"Oh, right." I totally forgot. "Well, I don't have anything else with me that's useful to you." The only thing that could be slightly of interest is Malou and there's no way in hell I'm going to barter her away. To some creepy stranger, no less.

The chevalier's continuous smile is unnerving. It's as if he knows these are just excuses. "Oh, I don't think that's true." He leans in and whispers, "I only ask a favour of you."

I think I'm going to be sick. There's only one kind of favour I can think of at the moment and it makes me want to puke. "A favour?" My voice is awfully thin.

"Yes, there's a group of people who are blocking a corridor not too far from here. I need you to get them to leave."

Okay? For a moment, the relief that he doesn't have a dirty mind lets me breathe easier. But I'm confused. "You want *me* to evict a bunch of squatters in the catacombs?"

"Not a bunch of squatters. Ghosts."

# CHAPTER 15

"**G**hosts?" I ask in a high-pitched voice.

Immediately, I clamp down on my mouth. I can't let Gaspar find out about it like this. My stomach turns at the thought of his inevitable disbelief.

"This is ridiculous," I manage to spit out. I don't know where my head is at. The only thing I can think of is that I need to get away from this man. And so, I march right off. I'm not even at the stairs before I start running.

My heart is thrashing in my chest while I rush down the stairs, trying my best not to fall in my blind panic. While my first thought was for Gaspar, the realisation that the chevalier knows hits me suddenly. Is he like me? Can he see ghosts? He didn't react to Emily at all. Perhaps it's all a perverse joke to him. Perhaps that's what cataphiles do to newbies like me.

I reach the ground, push past a worried Gaspar, and plunge into the crowd. The panic is blinding me and I continually stumble into people—none of them alive. Outraged complaints are calling out after me, but none of the ghosts bother with me for long. They all have more important things to do.

Just then, someone grabs me from behind and I let out a squeal.

To my dismay, it's the chevalier who caught up with me. "You don't need to run away from me."

The ghosts part around us, creating a tear-shaped space for us. "I'm not interested." Where is Gaspar? Is he upset about what he overheard? Or did the chevalier assault him? "What did you do to my boyfriend?"

The chevalier's eyebrows rise. "Your boyfriend?" He scoffs slightly, somehow amused about the notion. "Not much help, that one, is he?" My chest turns ice cold. "I'm sure he'll join you in a minute. In the meantime, let's talk about your… special talent."

I swallow heavily, trying hard not to let my thoughts get away from me. Gaspar is fine. He has to be. Meanwhile, I need to get rid of the chevalier. "I don't have a special talent."

"Oh please. You're telling me you don't see all the ghosts around you?"

That takes me by surprise. "You know?" I whisper. For fifteen years now, I've seen ghosts, and I've never met anyone like me. I don't know how to feel about the fact that the only other person who might share my talent is this creep.

The chevalier's smile widens. "You're not the first ghost whisperer to be drawn to the catacombs. So, now that's that dealt with. Will you take my proposal?"

I stare at him, dumbfounded. My brain seems lost for a minute, but then the thoughts crash into me. "No!" I try to jerk my hand away.

His grip hardens as his smile slips away, leaving only cold determination behind. Then he raises his other hand and pushes something between my clenched fingers. A folded piece of paper. "Think about it." At last, he lets go of me. "See you around, Alix."

I'm tempted to let the paper fall, but my curiosity prevails over my defiance, and I stuff the paper into my purse instead. My teeth are chattering and I suddenly feel cold. What have I got myself into? And where is Gaspar?

Emily finds me first. "I'm sorry," she whispers. "I shouldn't have involved you. You—"

Through the throng of people, I suddenly catch sight of Gaspar's soft brown mop of hair. "Gaspar!"

He looks as relieved as I feel when our eyes lock. I barely have time to glare at Emily before he pulls me into his arms and crushes me to his chest so hard I'm afraid for Malou. But her bag gets jostled to the side, and while she doesn't appreciate the movement, she'll be fine. More than I am.

"I lost you. I really thought I lost you!"

"I'm sorry!" I cry out, clawing at his back. "The ghosts and the chev—" I swallow a gasp. Gaspar can't find out like this. I need him now. "He frightened me."

Gaspar pulls me even tighter. "I'm so sorry, Alix. I should've never let you go up alone to him. I thought he was just a weirdo, not... whatever he is."

The word weirdo hits me wrong. I've heard it applied to me too many times. Especially because of the whole ghost thing. The danger has passed for now, but eventually I will need to fess up to Gaspar and it won't be pretty. It never is. There's no way I can deal with that now, so I just hold on to him and beg him to take me back up.

Gaspar complies without a question. He leads me back down the corridors to the Banga, which we both cross this time as we're both too exhausted to do the whole piggybacking thing again. I get wet to my waist, but at least the cold is keeping me awake.

Malou wakes up around the time we take a dinner break—or whatever time it is right now. I feed her, then fit her with her harness to let her stretch her legs. Seeing her little button eyes takes away some of the terror from my encounter with the chevalier.

"Cute," Gaspar comments. It's the first real word he's spoken since we left the Crossroad of the Dead behind.

"Yes." I'm just as drained.

When we finally make it outside, night has fallen. Unlike last time, there's no magical sea of lights. Clouds have descended and, judging by the shimmering puddles on the ground, it has rained. It starts up again before we reach the nearest Métro station. It's only there I find out that it's close to one o'clock.

I take out my phone and find several messages and missed calls from my family. Lacking the energy for a more elaborate answer, I just write them I'm on my way home.

"Do you want me to bring you home?" Gaspar asks, nodding at my message. "If not, I need to switch to the 7 at La Fayette."

"That's all right." I no longer need him to guide me, though my mother probably wouldn't be too happy about me being on the streets alone this late at night. It strikes me then that Gaspar should've offered to take me home, not asked if he was excused. "We're good, aren't we?" The fear in me rears its ugly head. Have I ruined this beautiful thing we had the moment I blurted out ghosts? Is he running from me now?

With a gentle smile, Gaspar leans over and kisses me on the hair. "Of course we are."

Despite his gesture, the bad feeling doesn't settle. "Can we talk? Not now, but tomorrow?"

He seems hesitant at first, but nods. "Yes. Let's do that."

I ask him to pick me up at the Panthéon after my shift and he kisses me once more. This one feels much better, easing my qualms. But before I can fully relax, he has to hop out. I lean back and sigh. Tomorrow won't be easy. I'm dreading our talk, though I know it's necessary. The ghosts are too big a part of my life to hide their existence. Once I'm no longer exhausted, I will find a way to break it to him in a way that won't mean he'll abandon me.

To keep myself from falling asleep, I play with Malou, who's the only one unbothered by the whole adventure. Though she's tiny, it feels good to have her with me. Sometimes, I wish I had a coat of spikes that I could use to protect my heart. Life would be so much easier then.

Just before my stop rolls around, I remember the piece of paper the chevalier gave me. Curiously, I take it out of the bag and unfold it in my lap. Malou walks right over it, but she can't obscure what it is. A map.

For a moment, I get excited. Did he give me the map I wanted after all? Then I realise that what I've got in my hands is far too small. The edges are ripped, indicating that I only got a piece of the map. A sign of goodwill then? Or just proof that he has what I want?

I'm so intrigued I almost miss my stop. I grab Malou, my backpack, and the map, and rush to the door before it's locked again, and the train continues moving. Because of my lack of awareness, I don't see Emily until I run into her.

"Gee!" I shout, almost losing my balance and falling back into the train. Panicked, I check my surroundings, but the few passengers who exited with me are already halfway up the stairs. "What are you doing here? And what were you thinking sending me down there?"

Emily casts down her eyes before defiantly raising them again. "I wouldn't have asked you if it wasn't important."

"Right." Her daughter. "A warning of what I'm getting myself into, though, would've been nice."

"I'm sorry. I didn't know you'd go straight to le Chevalier d'Os."

I cross my arms, not appreciating her accusing tone after she was the one who sent me into the catacombs in the first place. "Apparently, he's the one with the maps."

"He's not the only one."

"Well, he's the one we got." I unwrap my arms again to show her the map he's given me. "Is Ossa Arida on here?"

Emily glances at the map. "Of course not." She takes a deep breath, then pushes her finger onto another room. "But I'm pretty sure that's the room he wants you to clear of ghosts."

"Why?" I check the room and do a double take. "La Boutique de la Psychose?" If there ever was an ominous name, this is it. "What does he want? Why are the ghosts even bothering him?" Unless he's like me, he can go through any room he likes.

Emily takes her finger off and shrugs. "I don't know."

Frustration wells up in me. I know I'm tired when tears spring to my eyes. "Of course you don't. You don't know anything useful."

She pouts, but she doesn't refute me. "I'm new to this, remember? The catacombs are a bit of ghost central. There are complicated hierarchies I haven't got the hang of yet. I've just heard the chevalier talk about reclaiming the boutique. Why he needs you for that, I don't know."

"Well, this doesn't work." I push past her and go up the stairs. After tonight, I feel like my curiosity regarding the catacombs has been sated. Or rather, fear has replaced it.

"The others said you'd help a ghost in need."

I stop on top of the stairs and glare at her. "Who are the others?"

"Monsieur Marchand. He said you helped him recover his displaced finger bone."

The ghost she speaks of was one of my most surreal favours. Monsieur Marchand is a lovely old gentleman who frequents Cimetière Montmartre, and inspired my first foray into grave-digging. He's an artist who died horribly in a train accident. Due to the nature of the accident, not all of his bones had been found before burial. So I spent three days searching for the little bone he was so desperately missing in a field near the train tracks, then did a nerve-wracking late-night job of burying it under a bit of grass on top of his grave. It worked. He spends all the sunny days at the cemetery painting now. The paintings never last, but he's achieved a state of serenity that is enviable.

*"He* sent you my way?" My heart softens upon hearing his name. It reminds me that these ghosts don't have anyone else who understands how much these little things mean to them.

Emily nods. "He spoke highly of you."

I hug myself. "How dangerous is le Chevalier d'Os?"

"He's a madman." Emily spits out. "But I can lead you past the Crossroad of the Dead. He'll never know that you came back."

"You'll lead me?" I raise my eyebrows. Last time we spoke, she refused to do that until after the Crossroad of the Dead. It's the only reason I walked right into the chevalier's arms.

Emily chews her lip, looking disgruntled. "I was afraid to be seen. Then I remembered I was dead." She rolls her eyes and winces, the pain clear in her face. "Still new to this." Her eyes harden. "You don't need a map from him. I'll lead you. Please."

With a sigh, I give her a nod. The catacombs are huge. What are the chances of me running into him if I stay away from his base? It's not like he'll be in the catacombs day and night. "I will need a few days to prepare, but I'm willing to give it one more try. For your daughter."

"Thank you!" If I hadn't been convinced before, the relief on her face seals the deal. "You really are the best whisperer in town."

That's right. There are others like me. A fact withheld from me by all the ghosts I've helped and known. Especially one. Victor Hugo will have a lot to explain when I see him at work tomorrow.

# CHAPTER 16

It's half-past one when I finally arrive back home. Everyone seems to be asleep, so I take great care to be quiet, which is a challenge in itself in an old apartment like ours. I put some water in the sink for Malou to bathe in and use the toilet after holding it in for so long.

A look in the mirror tells me that I need a shower. So much for being all quiet. But I'd rather not risk getting an infection from that muddy Banga water. I dry Malou's feet and carry her into my room before I get myself ready.

Someone's waiting in my room, giving me a huge scare. "Hélène!"

"Took you long enough," my sister greets me. She's ready for bed but sitting at the desk with only the small light on. She points it at me, as if this were a police procedural and I'm under investigation. "Gosh, look at you."

"What are you doing here?" I know that I look like shit. That doesn't give her the right to invade my room and lie in wait with another sermon. "Shouldn't you be at home with your fiancé?"

Her lips become a thin line. "He's at work. Also, he's looking for you. In the *catacombs.*"

The thought of Cédric looking for me anywhere makes me shudder. "What?" I try to control my breathing. To help with that, I carry Malou to her cage and refill her food bowl as if it doesn't completely unnerve me that my sister sent her police fiancé after me as soon as she read the note I left.

Officer Cédric is a cataflic. Of course, he is.

"Because we were all worried sick when you didn't reply to our texts."

"I *did* reply."

"After midnight!"

The accusation in her voice stings. "I'm an adult, Hélène. Stop mothering me." If she hadn't prematurely read my note, everyone would have been at peace. Now they all got upset for nothing.

Hélène gasps. Her face gets all twisted, and I can see that the anguish is real. She was worried about me. "Alix, how could you do something so reckless? Do you have any idea of how dangerous this place is? They're not off-limits for no reason. Going into the catacombs by yourself is... unbelievable."

"I wasn't by myself. I was with my boyfriend."

"Right. The boyfriend you never told me about."

She's being ridiculous, and she doesn't even realise it. "If I were you, I would ask myself why." Anything to stop her from questioning me about the catacombs.

Hélène closes her eyes and takes a deep breath. "Why? Please, Alix, tell me why." It sounds exasperated.

If she wants honest answers, she can have one. I'm too tired to navigate this minefield. "You're barely here anymore. You're so busy with your career and your new lifestyle that you're simply not the first person I tell things to anymore. And honestly, I met him two weeks ago."

"And that's good enough to let him guide you through the catacombs? You hardly know him."

I laugh at her. "That's rich. You've been with Cédric for two years, and yet you've already moved in and are getting married."

"Two years is not insanely fast."

"Neither is spending some time together on an adventure."

Hélène breathes through her teeth, grasping for her usual calm. Her gaze gets stuck on my pants. "An adventure. Did you fall into the underground lake?" She only seems to realise their condition now.

After hours of walking, the pants are mostly damp now, but my socks still squelch a little when I move.

Hélène gets to her feet. "It's a lie, right? The boyfriend? You've been down there doing ghost stuff."

She hits the nail right on the head with the last bit, but the first part doesn't sit well with me. "I've got a boyfriend. You can ask Odile and Gaby about it."

Hélène winces when I remind her that these two are much better informed about my life. But that's her own fault.

"And I *was* with him."

"On ghost business."

When I don't reply, Hélène lets out an exasperated little gasp. Her worried gaze roves over my face and then down to my pants. "You need help, Alix."

I stare at her. The words slam into my face as if she's slapped me.

"Just look at you," Hélène continues, not realising how she's twisting the knife deeper with each word. "You crawl over cemeteries, dig up graves, and now you enter the catacombs at night. You've got no regard for your safety or health. And all because the *ghosts* tell you to."

"They don't tell me. They ask me."

Her voice cracks. "That's the same thing. I know you hate me for it, but I'm worried about you. You need help. Real help." Tears are streaming over her cheeks now.

Weirdly, her unfiltered show of emotion calms me. "Yes, and I'm getting help. From Gaby. And Gaspar." Not that he knows we've been following a ghost's lead yet. "People who believe me instead of trying to tell me what's real or not."

"Some would call it enabling." Hélène's lips are shaking as the venom leaves her mouth.

I'm stunned. A pain builds in my chest that makes each breath sting like a thousand needles. I want to lash out, to scream, to storm out. Anything to alleviate this pain.

Meanwhile, Hélène is already pushing her feelings down again. She slaps on a smile, but there's a craziness in her eyes that betrays the effort it costs her. Her hand brushes my arm. "All right, let's get you cleaned up first and make sure you get some sleep. And then in the morning, we can look at doctors together."

It's as if my opinion doesn't exist. My big sister always knows better, and I've got to fall in line or get left behind. Well, not anymore. I don't need Hélène to navigate life. "When I wake up, you'd better be gone," I whisper.

"Excuse me?"

"You heard me, Hélène. I'm sick of you smothering me. You used to believe me. Now I'm nothing more than an inconvenience to you. My ticks don't fit in your picture-perfect world."

Hélène stares at me as if I've become the ghosts she so detests. "Of course, I believed you when we were kids. But most people grow out of their fantasies. You doubled down on them. It's not healthy." If she was worried before, she seems angry now. "Cédric says the same thing. I don't know how you can't see that."

"You told Cédric?"

She crosses her arms and looks down her nose at me. "I tell him everything. He's going to be my husband."

"But not mine!" Rage overcomes me, and the urge to get physical gets worse. "You had no right to tell him! Absolutely no right."

Before I can get too deep into it, the door opens behind me, and my mother's head appears. "Alix. You're home. That's good. We'll talk in the morning, okay? In the meantime, could you two keep it down a bit?"

"No problem. Hélène was just going." I glare at my sister, daring her to protest.

A vein pulses on her forehead. The perfect mask is close to cracking again. "This is my home, too."

"Not anymore."

"Alix!" Maman is aghast. She checks with Hélène, who rolls her eyes at my apparent dramatics.

My sister walks over to where she's left her clothes and bag next to the spare bed. "You're clearly too emotional to talk, so I'll check in with you another time."

"Don't bother."

This time, she ignores me, but I can't be that mature. As soon as she's left my room, I slam the door shut behind me.

In the corridor, I can hear Maman and her talking. I know that they'll form a united front against me. Once that front was Hélène and me, but I'm no longer the one who has her ear. Officer Cédric is. And he knows about my ghosts.

# CHAPTER 17

F ortunately for me, Hélène has gone home by the time I get up. I ignore the deafening silence at breakfast. Papa and Odile have definitely heard about the fight but decide to stay out of it. Maman watches me the entire time, as if she's trying to find the cracks in my well-functioning mask. There is no mask. I'm already stripped bare, but she and Hélène refuse to acknowledge that. At least, she doesn't hand me a stack of psych brochures, as feared.

I escape any planned conversations by having to rush to work. When I jump on my bicycle, my body takes its vengeance on me for not giving it enough rest. After the fight with Hélène, I still had to wash myself, and then I couldn't get to sleep for ages. In the end, I've slept only a little more than four hours, and it shows. The people taking my tours today will probably be bored to death.

While I help Philippe get the mausoleum ready for opening, I call Gaby. I need my best friend right now.

As it turns out, Gaby was still sleeping, but one quick rundown of my nasty fight and she's wide awake. "That bitch! Sorry, Alix, but I'm actually impressed you didn't scratch her eyes out."

"It was a close call." I don't really get physical, but Hélène knows how to push all my buttons. A sister thing, I suppose. "I just can't believe she would tell Officer Cédric."

"Me neither." At least Gaby is just as outraged. It makes me feel a little bit better about how I handled the late-night altercation. "I get confiding in your spouse about your family, but this is so personal. Especially with the conclusions she's drawn. I don't know. I would have talked to *you* about it, not him."

Anxiously, I pull my lip between my teeth. "But you don't need to talk to me because you believe me, right?"

"Duh!" Relief floods me at the instant rebuttal. "Is it disconcerting when you see something I can't? Of course, but you've proven ghosts are real to me so many times I have to believe you."

"Thanks." It means the world to me that there's at least one living person whom I can share my affliction with. And maybe after tonight, there will be two. "I'm going to tell Gaspar after work."

"Are you sure?" Gaby sounds everything but. "It's a bit early."

"For the truth?" I remind myself of how he pressed my body against his after he thought he'd lost me. He might not have confided all his fears and pain in me yet, but he deeply cares for me. "I need to tell him. Now, before I get too attached." Now, while the hurt after a rejection will still be bearable.

On the other line, Gaby sighs. "I guess you're right. It's the mature thing to do, for sure. I just..." Another deep breath. "I love this current you. Going out with your boyfriend, trying new things, being in love. Not saying it will end. If Gaspar is even the slightest bit as cool as you make him sound, he's going to be on board. I'm just wary of the possibility he isn't."

She isn't the only one who's wary about that. I wish I could confidently say that he'd be fine with it, but after meeting the chevalier, the weird mood on our ride home, and the wounds Hélène tore open with her well-meaning but condescending concern, I'm not so sure either. "Well, better now than later."

Meanwhile, the doors have opened, and Philippe has issued the first tickets. A few people are gathering at the tour sign. "I'll call you afterwards, okay?"

"Yes, please! And don't let Hélène get into your head. She's Officer Cédric's creature now."

I'm not sure if it was supposed to be funny, but I don't find the prospect encouraging at all. After last night, I'm still mad at Hélène, but she is my big sister. I don't want to lose her to Officer Cédric. With a sigh, I hang up and get myself ready for the tour.

It's a long day. I only survive the shift because of my ghosts. Victor is not happy with me after going against his explicit wishes, though I'm not really happy with him either. "You could've told me that it's like ghost central down there."

"And risk losing you to that world?" He watches me concerned. "Did you manage to complete the favour?"

"No. But I've got a lead."

He draws his bushy eyebrows together. "You're not going back, are you?"

At this point, I refuse to answer directly. "I need more information. Why are there so many ghosts down there?"

Victor clicks his tongue. "It's a commune. Look, the afterlife is very long. And not everyone is fortunate enough to hang out in such a prestigious place as this. Some ghosts are happy hanging around the living, clinging to life as if there was a way back, but the majority of us—*them*—want something new. If they have to hang around for decades or centuries after their death, they might as well have their own society. Their own... *life*. I suppose that's what's happening. A meaning to their existence." He nods at Rousseau. "You should speak with Jean about it. He considers himself an expert on the meaning of the afterlife."

I'm not sure I'm awake enough to listen to philosophy today. It's much more interesting what's happening down there. "So, instead of hanging out up here, they've built up their own commune below?" This is so cool. Metal, as Gaspar would say.

"If you can call it a functioning commune. Then again, when are commune generally functioning?" Century-old resignation seeps out of him.

"Do they have a government?" I want to know all there is about the ghost commune.

Victor raises his eyebrow. "The point of a commune is not to have a government. But I guess, as with every kind of human society, there is some form of leadership. Have you ever heard of Nexus?"

My heart skips a beat. He fully expects me not to, but I've heard of it. Gaspar mentioned it first to me, and Emily repeated it last night. They are a group of cataphiles who've dedicated their lives to mapping the catacombs and preserving its history. Le Chevalier d'Os is rumoured to be a part of them.

It's not what Victor says. "They are a group of ghosts who have created the commune, doing endless work in creating structures to ease ghosts into the afterlife. It's a noble vocation for sure, just not my... vibe, as you young people say nowadays."

I roll my eyes at him. Victor is worse than any boomer when it comes to using slang. I don't know why he even tries. "Nexus consists of ghosts?"

"Well, on our side, yes." He casts me a long look. Despite seeming a little disgruntled, he speaks on, "It is rumoured that Nexus is the connection between the dead and the living. Ghosts on our side. Ghost whisperers on your side."

"Ghost whisperers?" So it's true.

There are still visitors in the crypt, and a few glance at me warily. Pointing to my ear, I give them an awkward smile. "Podcast." We're all ignoring that I shouldn't listen to anything at work.

I glare at Victor and whisper-hiss at him, "So, there *are* others like me, and you never told me?" Inevitably, I have to think of the chevalier. He knew about the ghosts—and my abilities.

"Of course there are." Victor's face is full of sadness. "How do you think I knew what you were when we first met? However, there's no one quite like you."

"Oh, really?" I can't help it. Maybe it's Hélène's aggressive disbelief in ghosts or the fact that I've spent fifteen years wondering if I'm only imagining things because no one else could see what I did. My heart bleeds at the realisation I didn't necessarily have to go through all of this on my own.

Victor takes a step closer and puts his hand on my shoulder. The weight is real, just as it always has been. "Someone with your capability of compassion. The ghost whisperers I've met before you help sometimes, but never without ulterior motives. You rarely refuse anyone. Even if I wish you would sometimes."

"Like when it leads me into the catacombs?" I ask softly.

"Never more than then. I'm worried about you, kid. That's all." The difference between when Hélène said it and when he does is that he doesn't dismiss me in the same breath. Victor believes in me. He's worried for my safety, not worried I'm losing my mind.

"If something happens to you, it'll be my fault. I dragged you into this world."

I lean in to hug him, but remember at the last moment that people are still watching. He'll have to get the message through my eyes instead. "I'm beyond glad you did. My life has become so much more exciting since then."

When I *do* go back to the catacombs, it will be for more than just Emily. This time, I'm going back for me.

# CHAPTER 18

Surprisingly, I feel a lot better when I finish my shift. I was tired the whole time, but in the last half hour, I seemed to have got a second wind. Night owls for the win. It's either that, or my anxiety is flooding my veins with adrenaline.

Gaspar is waiting for me at the top of the stairs of the Panthéon, leaning against one of the classical columns with his hands in his pockets. The wind is tousling his hair as he stares into the distance. He seems cold and a bit lost—until the moment he sees me. Then his face blooms, his eyes sparkle, and he smiles while giving me a shy wave. "There you are."

"Here I am." Unfortunately, his smile doesn't do it for me today. I'm too nervous that it might be the last time I'll see him smiling at me.

We exchange kisses, and I ask him whether he wants to grab something to eat. After the long shift, I'm starving. Plus, it gives me an excuse to skip my family's dinner and avoid the aftermath of Hélène's intervention.

His smile falters. "Can we walk instead?"

Odd, and not at all comforting. There are very few reasons why the French would refuse a dinner date, especially when the weather isn't all that inviting. I'm not liking my chances here. Still, it has to be done. Gaspar deserves the truth about last night and my sudden interest in the catacombs. Unless he breaks things off before I even get to it.

To calm my nerves a little and to make a point about it being dinnertime, I buy a savoury crêpe with eggs, ham, and cheese from the crêperie across from the Panthéon. Gaspar chuckles softly but doesn't join me.

"So, where are we going?" I ask before taking a bite and burning my tongue on the hot cheese.

He shrugs. "Anywhere is good." Fortunately, he follows up his lacklustre answer by walking down the road toward the Seine.

The wind helps cool the crêpe, and soon I'm able to enjoy the simple mix of salt, dough, and cheese. Gaspar doesn't insist on talking while I'm eating, instead keeping his thoughts to himself.

By the time the last scrap of food has settled in my stomach, we arrive at the water, which is as grey as the sky today. On the other side of the bridge, the tall towers of Notre Dame rise on the Île de la Cité. We turn away from the sight to walk the footpath on the shoreline. On sunny days, it's packed with tourists and little stallholders, but at this time of day, and with the heavy grey clouds hanging so low, it's rather deserted.

I glance mournfully at a packed restaurant. Though not hungry anymore, I yearn for the warmth and joyous company. I would prefer Gaspar's company to either, but he still hasn't spoken a word. Time to rip off the bandage. "You're going to break up with me, aren't you?" If he does, I can spare myself the embarrassment of talking about my ghosts.

Gaspar startles. "What? No!" His head whips around to me, his eyes wide. "That is the last thing I want to do. I like being with you. You..." His face softens. "Did you think I was going to break up with you?"

Relief washes over me, but it taints so quickly I hiccup. Gaspar wants to be with me, but now that I know it's not him, the fear I'm gonna lose him anyway is too much to bear. Tears form in my eyes.

Without a moment's hesitation, Gaspar wraps me in his arms and pulls me close. "I'm sorry. I didn't mean for you to think I was planning to break up with you. There's just been so many changes in my life that I've only barely begun wrapping my head around, and yesterday brought up some stuff. It has nothing to do with you, though." He kisses my forehead, then rubs the tears from my cheeks with his thumbs. "I'm not letting you go that easily."

It's sweet, yet doesn't help in the least. "Last night..."

"Was pretty messed up. I agree." He's suddenly so vehement, as if he'd been tuned out until the memory came back to him. "I never should've taken you to that creep. The catacombs were always something of a fun adventure to me—a dare—and a place for good music. But I've ignored the dark side. And that stupid chevalier is definitely not good people. My heart stopped when he went after you. I'm so sorry I pulled you into my mess."

The memory of le Chevalier d'Os grabbing my wrist comes back to me, making me shudder. Everything about our interaction was frightening, but it was my fault, not Gaspar's. I sling my arms around him and bury my nose in his hoodie, as if that will help. "I'm the one pulling you into my mess."

Gaspar blinks in confusion. "What do you mean?"

"I can see ghosts," I mumble. When there's no reaction, I reckon that he didn't hear me. Perhaps I shouldn't start with such a deep dive-in.

I gather my courage and glance up at him, wetting my lips. "I'm going to tell you something really outlandish." His eyebrows start crawling up, and my stomach turns. "You will probably think I've completely lost my mind and run for it, but..."

Gaspar's face relaxes, and a lazy smile curls his lips. "Try me."

"Okay." I don't trust his confidence in the least. "So, the reason I wanted a map of the catacombs has nothing to do with my historical interest. Don't get me wrong. I love the catacombs, and I can't wait to explore more of it. But I went there because someone asked me to retrieve something for them. Something they lost in Ossa Arida."

My words make him frown. Of course, they do. "If they lost something this far deep in the catacombs, why do they need *you* to get it for them?"

And here comes the hard part. "Because they're already dead." To make it easier for him, I let go of our embrace.

He's still struggling to follow me. "So, was it in their will or?"

"No. I..." I have to take a deep breath before I can even attempt to get the first information out again. "I only met them after their death. As a ghost. I can see ghosts."

"What?" Gaspar's face goes slack.

The urge to cry is powerful again, but with the wind and a lot of blinking, I manage to keep my tears at bay. "I know it sounds outrageous. You probably don't believe ghosts are real, but I've been seeing ghosts since I was a child. They come to me with all kinds of requests." I don't know why I keep talking. From the looks of it, I've already lost him. "There is proof. I mean, I know things I'm not supposed to know. Like Ossa Arida. Never read about that place in any of the books."

"Wait, stop." Gaspar holds up a hand. "What do you mean you can see ghosts? Like spiritual energy or Halloween ghosts?"

I shake my head. "No, to me, ghosts appear just like normal people. I can even touch them. They feel alive to me, but I'm the only one who can."

"How do you know they're dead then?" he asks almost aggressively.

I'm taken aback. I expected ridicule, sure, but not this line of questioning? It takes me a moment to gather myself. "Because people like Victor Hugo or Marie Curie are well known to be dead."

I shouldn't have brought up the famous ghosts. Gaspar takes a step back, shaking his head. "Right."

"What I mean is, it's pretty obvious sometimes by the way they dress, speak, or behave. Sometimes it's less obvious and gets really embarrassing because I *don't* know they're a ghost until people around me notice I'm talking to myself or act all-around weird, but that's another clue. I can see ghosts." The last bit comes out defiantly. Still raw from my fight with Hélène, I'm no longer willing to hide what I am. At least not when I've already told him so much. There's no going back on it, anyway.

"No." Seems like I'm not the only one defiant. "That's crazy. There's no such things as ghosts. It doesn't make sense. You're either dead or alive." He swallows, still shaking his head. "I've got to go."

"Of course, you do." I try not to feel anything, but I'm kidding myself. Each of Gaspar's words has cut me open. I'm bleeding out in front of him, but he no longer cares.

"I'll call you." He hesitates. "Maybe."

The killing blow.

I don't attempt to change his mind. If there is even the slightest chance of him coming around, he'll do it after having time to himself. Not that I have any hope the way he's reacted. We're done. The only saving grace is that, since we don't share any classes or other activities, I'll probably never catch him rolling his eyes at me.

Gaspar strides off, leaving me behind fast, while I'm frozen to the spot, unable to take my eyes off his back, even after I can no longer see him.

# CHAPTER 19

Two hours later, I'm standing in front of Gaby's door, drenched from head to toe. I've been wandering the city aimlessly after Gaspar abandoned me, my head empty, not even noticing when it had started raining. I have no idea why I expected it to go any differently this time. It never has before. Well, apart from one time.

"Oh, darling!" Gaby greets me after opening the door. "You poor thing. Come on in." She drags me inside. "I've got wine."

Gaby got her own place after her parents left the city behind and moved further south where the weather was warmer and the rent cheaper. Her apartment isn't much bigger than a shoe box. It used to be a servant's bedroom when the building was owned by a rich Victorian-era family; now it's been turned into tiny apartments. Hers is a single room with a bed, a desk, some creative storage space, the tiniest kitchen in the world, and a shower in the corner, hidden by a narrow wardrobe from the rest of the room.

That's where Gaby jockeys me towards first. "Have you eaten?"

"I…" My mind is blank. "I think so."

"I'll reheat some onion soup and cut up some bread and cheese while you shower."

She doesn't wait for my affirmation and busies herself in the kitchen less than a metre away. I have no qualms undressing in the corner, though it takes me quite some time to peel the wet clothes from my skin. Hard to believe we had spring-like temperatures only last week. If today's weather is any indication, winter is definitely on its way.

As soon as I step into the shower, I moan. I take care not to use too much hot water at first, but even lukewarm it's such a revelation against my ice-cold skin. Gaby puts on a playlist, her French-pop favourites, and sings loudly along to Christine & the Queens as she heats up the food. Both the water and Gaby's joyful presence start to thaw my frozen heart.

When I've finally dried up, Gaby awaits me on her bed. She has this half table, half tray that allows her to eat in the comfort of her bed. On the tray are two bowls of soup, some fresh baguette, butter, and a small selection of cheeses. A bottle of red wine and two glasses complement the food.

I throw on a pair of Gaby's pyjamas and carefully climb into bed next to her, then dip a slice of bread in the onion soup and take a bite. Salty and savoury are exactly what I need right now. For a few precious moments, I allow myself to savour the rich food and not think of anything else but how the flavours meld on my tongue, and are enhanced by the fruity note of the wine when I drink.

Then my phone buzzes, and my heart skips a beat. Gaby climbs out of our cocoon to grab it from my bag. Her face quickly squashes my hopes that it could be Gaspar. "Your maman."

Of course. They'd be waiting with dinner at home. I can't remember if I ever sent her a text to go ahead and eat.

"Don't worry. I've got this." She drops my phone on the blankets, pulls out her own, and quickly types a couple of messages. "All right, that's settled."

Curious, I watch her as she climbs back in. "Who did you write?" I know that she's got the numbers of at least half my family, if not all of them. She's even part of the second family chat.

"Odi. Told her you're with me. That you're having boy trouble and that she needs to look after Malou for you, because you're staying with me tonight."

I wrap my arms around Gaby and rest my cheek on her shoulder. "You're the best."

Despite her message, my phone buzzes again with a message from Maman: "Are you okay, chérie?"

With a sigh, I force myself to reply to her. "Don't worry. I'm fine." After the night at the catacombs, she probably wants to hear from me directly.

"Take care of yourself." A heart emoji completes the message. For now, I seem to have calmed her enough to leave me be. After Hélène's intervention, there will be a reckoning, though. Probably when I feel least prepared to deal with it.

Frustrated, I pour myself another glass of red wine and sip at it while I nibble on a piece of Comté, barely registering the nutty flavour.

When the food is finished, Gaby puts the tray away but keeps the wine glasses at hand. She crosses her legs on top of the blanket, facing me. "All right, tell me all about it, so I can practice my rant against Gaspar."

Even though it shouldn't be a laughing matter, I have to giggle. However, as soon as I call back the memories to form an answer, the giggle dies on my lips. "He got really angry."

"Angry?" Gaby sounds outraged on my behalf.

"I don't know why. Maybe he thought I was making fun of him or he's afraid of ghosts or..."

"He's a jerk like most men?" Gaby throws me a pointed stare, then takes another sip from her glass. "How dare he get angry at you when you confide in him? When you're vulnerable?"

"I love you," I whisper, in awe of how vehemently she defends me against anyone.

Gaby giggles. "Of course you do. I'm your best friend. So, what do we do? Do we send some ghosts to haunt him?"

"He wouldn't notice them."

She rolls her eyes. "So annoying."

"We don't do anything. I should have never told him." It was too early in our relationship. He didn't trust me yet.

But Gaby won't have it. "Uh-uh. No, if he reacted like this, you're better off without him. You've pulled off the band-aid; he turned out to be an ass. Now you can move on and find someone better."

All the beautiful memories we made in such a short time come back to me at the thought of who could be better than Gaspar, pre-ghost confession. Even the scary ones, down at the Crossroad of the Dead, fill me with warmth. The way he pressed my body against his, held me so tight I couldn't move, until my whole world just became his heartbeat, his breath, his heat, is a tough one to leave behind.

"Oh, ma puce!" Gaby leans over to her nightstand and plucks a tissue from the box, so I can wipe my cheeks. "You will find someone better."

"I don't want to," I manage to croak out. "Gaspar was... I don't know how anyone could be better than that."

"Well, they could be supportive of your ghost-sight for a start."

I wince at the mention of what cost me this first boyfriend in a long time. "No one is. It's weird. It requires so much suspension of disbelief. Unless they can see ghosts themsel—"

A thought crosses my mind that is outrageous, so outrageous, I don't dare entertain it. It's not like I'm that eager—or desperate—to move on. However, I can't help but share my newest discovery with Gaby.

I sit up straight, mimicking Gaby's pose. "You won't believe what I found out yesterday."

Gaby picks up on my change in attitude, instantly intrigued. "Try me."

"All right. So, when we went into the catacombs last night, we met this guy. He's got this super ridiculous title: le Chevalier d'Os." Here in Gaby's bed, with a glass of wine in my hand, it sounds presumptuous.

"What?" Gaby sputters, almost spraying her bed with droplets of red wine. "They do larping down there?"

I shrug. "Whatever. He seems to be some big shot. We went to him because according to..." Nope, still too painful. "He's got maps. Anyway, so we approach him and he's instantly interested in me."

"Is he good-looking?"

"Gaby!" I playfully slap her knee. "No, he was a total creep. But!" I lick my lips, my eyes burning with a sudden fervour. "He asked me about my ghosts."

Her mouth drops open. "No way? Is he like you?"

I knew she would understand my excitement. "I don't know. Maybe. However, both Emily and Victor confirmed that there are other ghost whisperers in Paris."

"Wait." Gaby's eyelids flutter as she's trying to follow me. "Victor confirmed it?"

I nod.

"Victor Hugo?"

I nod again.

"The same Victor Hugo whom you've been friends with for two years now?"

I'm starting to see what she's getting at. "Yeah. I was pretty disappointed as well."

Gaby huffs. "Men!" She takes another swig from the glass. "All right. So, there are others like you. That's awesome! Gosh, you must be so relieved to discover that." I knew she would get me. "I know how hard this is for you. Especially with that cow Hélène messing with your head." She hasn't forgotten our earlier phone call yet. "I bet she'll be eating her words when she hears this."

"Slow down. I haven't found another ghost whisperer yet."

"Unless the chevalier..."

I shudder at the thought. "Anyone but him."

"Okay." Gaby determinedly nods her head. "So, how do we find you a nice ghost whisperer?"

It's obviously a dig at my recent relationship failure. "I don't want to replace Gaspar," I whisper. "He might still come around."

Gaby raises an eyebrow. "Fine. I wasn't on board instantly, either. But!" She points a finger at me. "I didn't shout at you. Nor did I run away."

"And that's why you're the best."

That mollifies her sufficiently. "I know. But fine, Gaspar gets a grace period. Perhaps he even manages to fix his phone in the meantime." She huffs, then draws herself up. "Still, how do we get you in touch with other ghost whisperers?"

"Well, apparently, a lot of them frequent the catacombs."

Instantly, Gaby deflates again. "You're not planning to go down again, are you?"

I don't lie to Gaby. "I promised Emily I'd try once more. She vowed to guide me this time." A bitter taste spreads on my tongue. "Which is fortunate because Gaspar will very likely not come around, so I'll be on my own."

"No way."

"Gaby, please. I know it's not exactly safe, but there are so many ghosts down there. You should've seen them. And history. So much history. Plus, I've promised to get that medallion for her daughter." And while Gaspar was also a part of the catacombs, they're so much bigger than him. "I belong down there."

Gaby puts her glass away and leans forward to take my hands into hers. "You belong up here with the living."

"The ghost whisperers are down there, too."

She sighs, her face pained. I notice how her breath is becoming more shallow. "All right. But you're not going alone. I'll come with you."

"You can't!" The suggestion horrifies me so much I crawl away from her. "You're claustrophobic. You'd hate the catacombs."

Gaby takes a deep breath and closes her eyes, already struggling with the idea. "Yes, there's that."

"I won't go then."

"Sure you will," Gaby calls me out. "Just when I'm not looking." She crosses her arms, then thinks better of it and relaxes them again. "Look, I'm not doing this to blackmail you into staying. I mean it. I don't want you alone down there, just with the ghosts. Remember what happened last time?"

"Last time?"

"When we did that favour for Josephine Baker?" She wipes her forehead as if she's already perspiring due to her fear. "I let you go into those walls alone because my claustrophobia held me back, and you almost got killed! So, no, I'm coming with you. Unless, of course, Gaspar has a change of heart."

And for a moment, we're both desperate to hold on to that hope.

But that's not going to happen. Tears well to the forefront and I can no longer keep them in. I throw myself at Gaby, almost tipping her over in the process. "What would I ever do without you?"

"A lot of stupid things." She tries to glare at me before bursting into laughter. "Though, apparently, I'm just as bad." She hugs me back.

I notice after a while that she's holding onto me tighter and tighter. "You're okay?"

"Your ghost knows the way, right?"

"She was an experienced catacomb tour guide," I assure her.

Gaby takes a shaky breath, then plasters on a big smile. "All right. Let's get to planning, then, shall we? And shopping. We'll need proper clothes, plus camping gear or something, assuming it'll take us longer than a few hours. Food, water. We can't forget about Malou. She did save your life in the Dordogne after all."

The sudden enthusiasm with which she launches herself into this new adventure is infectious. It fills my heart with hope and determination. As much as it hurts losing Gaspar, he's only been a blip in my life against Gaby's steadfast presence. There's no one I'd rather have with me than my best friend.

# CHAPTER 20

When I return home after Monday's classes, my grace period is up. Maman corners me in the hallway before I even get my shoes off. "Can we talk? I've made macarons."

"To bribe me?"

She laughs, but it turns into a sigh. "I feel like tough talks always go down better with sweets."

"So that's why we always have cookies around." I don't like the idea of a tough talk, but perhaps I can lighten the mood enough to ensure she won't believe Hélène's lies.

Once again, she smiles at my joke, then nods towards the living room. "Papa is still at the office. He's got a deadline to meet by tomorrow or so, and Odile is out with her friends."

"So, it's just you and me?"

The way my mother pulls on her lip with her teeth doesn't bode well. "Hélène wants to join us. She's coming over right after work."

The mood is suddenly a lot darker. "I don't want her here."

"Alix." My mother sighs in exasperation. "She's your sister. I want her here."

"So the two of you can gang up on me?" I go back to my shoes. "Maybe I should move to Gaby's then."

"Don't be ridiculous. No one is ganging up on anybody."

I cross my arms, not convinced. "You're going to tell me that you haven't set this up with Hélène and that you're not trying to tell me I'm insane and need urgent psychiatric help?"

Maman visibly deflates. "We're worried about you."

"There's nothing to be worried about!" I don't shout at my mother like I did at Hélène, but I'm hurt all over again.

My mother was the first one I told about the ghosts. When it first happened, she took me in her arms and held me tight, but she listened. It wasn't until several years later when she suddenly set me up with a child psychiatrist to discuss my ongoing grief that I found out the whole time she'd thought it was my coping mechanism to deal with the death of my grandmother, and she'd begun to worry because it lasted for so long.

She'd never believed me.

"Your behaviour is becoming erratic," Maman says in that same calm manner Hélène has emulated perfectly. We still haven't moved into the dining room.

"Is it? I haven't missed a single class. I'm showing up at work, where I get lots of praise, my grades aren't slipping, I meet with

Gaby, I got a boyfriend. Sounds to me like I'm living a perfectly normal life." Only, there is no boyfriend anymore, because he couldn't handle the ghosts.

Maman swallows. There's a flash of confusion, as if she's only now realised that I'm not as erratic as Hélène has probably painted me. "Well, you went into the catacombs," she says almost cautiously.

"So do lots of people. Do you call them all insane, too?"

Her eyes widen. I realise she probably would call them insane, but at last, she concedes the point. "Then I'd have to call your Papa insane, so no. And for the record, I'm not calling you insane either."

"Wait, Papa goes into the catacombs?"

"Not anymore," she hurries to say. "He told me once that he'd done it a couple of times in his youth. Before we met."

I raise my eyebrows.

"Fine. He carried on a little longer and took me once, but I hated it."

Whatever line of attack my mother had planned with Hélène has crumbled before my sister even got here. "I see. So, what exactly makes my foray into the catacombs erratic? Seeing as my *boyfriend* took me there." It hurts to keep calling Gaspar that, but there's no way I'm going to talk about the break-up in the current ambush. Not when I've almost managed to defuse the situation.

Just then, a key rattles in the lock behind me. I tense and take a swift step towards the door of my room, as Hélène steps in.

"Oh, Alix. You beat me here," she says, chipper, as if we hadn't had a huge fight the last time we saw each other. When she leans in to exchange kisses, I jerk away. Her face falls. "You're still mad."

"Let's go sit down," my mother suggests. "We don't need to stand in the hallway like a bunch of vagabonds."

I would much rather escape to my room. In my opinion, I've cleared up all there was to clear up. No need to get into it once more with Hélène. But since she won't go away, I might as well have some homemade macarons.

My mother has done her usual variety of green pistachio and yellow salted caramel. Both of them are delicious; the shells crisp on the outside but gooey on the inside, while the filling is sweet but salty. I pick a pistachio one today, because I can't resist the vibrant green, while my mother pours some coffee for the three of us.

"Odi will be mad she's not part of this," I mutter between bites. I've never told my youngest sister about the ghosts, afraid she'd only use them for ammunition against me. Though it seems I had my sisters twisted around in that regard.

Hélène shoots me a dark look. "She gets into enough trouble without adopting yours."

"And again with the mothering."

"Maman," Hélène complains, uncharacteristically whiny. Even our mature older sister reverts to a child when alone with her family. At least, sometimes. "Will you tell her then?"

"We already had a chat." To my surprise, Maman is turning on Hélène. "You're both adults. You shouldn't come running to me to tattle on your sister. As for Alix." Her eyes find mine and some sort of understanding passes between us. "I trust that she's making informed decisions without taking too many risks."

I try to hide my smile behind the remnants of my macaron while Hélène's eyes bulge. Obviously, Maman is going off-script after our talk in the hallway.

"But the ghosts!" Hélène gestures at me.

"Don't seem to impact her day-to-day life in a concerning way."

The smile freezes on my lips despite my mother speaking in my favour. Everything I told her in the hallway was true. Everything but the thing about Gaspar. In truth, the ghosts have a huge impact on my life, both as active parts of it, like Victor and my other friends at the Panthéon, and by impairing my ability to form lasting human connections with living people. I wouldn't give up my power for anything in the world, but it'd be a lonely road if it weren't for Gaby and Malou.

Hélène crosses her arms. "What about the catacombs?"

Maman takes a deep breath. "As I said, informed decisions, as few risks as possible." Her voice is strained, the message clear. *Please be careful.*

"It's illegal!"

My mother waves her off. "Oh, please. They just don't want any tourists down there. When we went down there, the cataflics knew your father by name, checked we were good, and wished us a good night."

Hélène's jaw drops open. "You and Papa went down there too?"

"Before we had you." Maman still sounds so wonderfully unaffected that I can't help but smile. "As I understand it, Alix went there with her new beau." She smiles fondly at me all of a sudden. "I can't wait to meet him. Please invite him for dinner soon."

I force a big smile, then quickly take a sip from my cup. "Of course."

Maman leans back happily, but Hélène watches me with narrowed eyes. Whatever suspicion she has, she shakes it off, though. "I can't condone this."

"Enough." Maman glares at her. "Alix is old enough to make her own decisions. She hardly needs my approval. She certainly doesn't need yours. Now, stop this nonsense and be friends again."

But our fight was too hurtful for that. We both hurled words to wound at each other.

"I see." Hélène gets up. "I'd better get going then."

"Where are you going?" Maman asks in confusion.

Hélène grabs her handbag and replies stiffly. "Home. Since I'm obviously not welcome in this one anymore."

"That's not true." The hurt look on my mother's face is like a knife to my chest. She doesn't deserve such a low blow. It's me who Hélène feels ousted by. "Léni!"

My sister ignores the plea and vanishes in the hallway.

I heave a sigh, then get up on my feet. "I'll go and fix it." As much as I hate to be the one to make the first step, it's what I owe Maman for her advocacy and trust.

Dragging my feet, I catch Hélène as she slips into her shoes. "Who's being dramatic now?" Perhaps not the most diplomatic approach for the situation.

Hélène shoots me a withering glare. "Congrats. You got what you want. Maman's on your side now."

I cross my arms and lean against the wall. "There are no sides. You're the one who tried to pull her into this." This won't work. Something's got to give, and that something is me. "Look, I'm sorry for what I said the other day. It was a long night. I was cold and miserable and didn't expect you to ambush me in my room."

"It wasn't an ambush," Hélène says through her gritted teeth. "I was worried about you. Still am."

"I know." The words taste so bitter I scrunch up my nose. "I appreciate it... to a degree. But you went too far."

Hélène shakes her head. She grabs her scarf and wraps it around her neck. "Not far enough if you're going to keep endangering yourself." Her shoulders sag slightly. "Please don't go down there again. You don't know the horror stories Cédric told me about. It's an evil place."

A barrage of counterarguments floods my brain, but I manage to keep my mouth shut and nod curtly. I just need to make peace with Hélène, nothing more. "I'll keep that in mind."

"See that you do." Of course, she can't leave it at that. The oldest sister needs to be in control. The hierarchy has to be restored. She nods towards the living room. "Tell Maman I'm sorry, but I need some space."

"Will do."

Hélène nods sharply, then checks her handbag for the car keys, but finds something else instead, a pile of leaflets. She cautiously puts them on the shelf next to the door. "It doesn't hurt to look at them." And with that, she leans in to quickly peck my cheeks and leaves.

Everything inside of me is revolted by the leaflets on the shelf, but my curiosity wins over my instincts and I grab the pile. Psychiatrists. Therapies.

With a grunt, I stuff them into the bin. At this rate, Hélène should start looking for a new witness, because if this continues, I'm seriously considering giving her wedding a miss.

# CHAPTER 21

O ver the week, Gaby and I prepare everything for our trip into the catacombs. I request leave for my Sunday shift, and we buy sturdy boots and proper clothes, as well as some heavy-duty lamps and spares, a first-aid kit, and a pair of lightweight sleeping bags. All of it goes into my father's old camping backpack.

I'd hoped to be able to speak to him, but he's working on a big exposé at the moment and is barely home. If I *do* see him, it's only for a short meal before he heads off to sleep. It's a shame, because from the sounds of it, he knows the catacombs as well as Gaspar does.

Speaking of Gaspar. I've let him know of when I plan to go back in. First, by sending him a text, and then by leaving him a note in the catacombs book in the library. He hasn't tried to make contact all week, and as Friday draws nearer, I resign myself to the fact that he won't come back.

Hélène would feel vindicated if she hears of it. Once more, ghosts came in between me and my relationship, but no more. This weekend, I will find other ghost whisperers and finally make the connections I so crave.

I keep my promise to my mother by doing my due diligence and reading everything I can find about the catacombs. No one leaves behind detailed information, but I manage to glean important insights about what to expect from obscure blogs and forum entries. I even manage to obtain a map. It isn't very detailed and is mighty confusing as to what levels the drawn streets are on, but it puts the main avenues into relation to the above-ground grid. While I don't find Ossa Arida on it, I should be able to orient myself underground with the help of the signs I've seen.

One thing keeps standing out, though. The catacombs are no place for anyone who's claustrophobic.

You cannot panic underground. If the reports are to be believed, it would be the worst-case scenario. Gaby and I will have to climb down wells that are twenty metres deep. A long climb, and an even longer fall if you slip. And once at the bottom, it's vital that you stay calm, even if you get lost—something that apparently happens to every cataphile at least once. *Especially* if you get lost. And then there are the windows one has to squeeze through sometimes.

I can't take Gaby. Not because she'd be a burden to me, but because I don't want to risk her getting hurt. Only problem is that she won't let me go alone.

*Don't take too many risks.* That was the second piece of advice Maman gave me.

So on Friday, I do the one thing I thought I'd never do. I lie to Gaby.

"He called," I tell her excitedly when we meet for Research Methods in the lab.

Gaby stares at me, dumbfounded for a moment, then her eyes widen. "Did he come around?"

I nod, giving the performance of my life by bopping in my seat and smiling from ear to ear. Even my hormones are tricked by my facial muscles, and serotonin floods me. "Yes. We talked for hours last night. He apologised profusely and asked how to make it up to me. He feels horrible." As he should. And very likely never will.

It turns my stomach to lie to Gaby, but this is for her safety. She'd become more and more nervous by the hour, as if we're heading for Doomsday, not an exciting adventure.

Since Gaby's never met Gaspar, there's no chance of him blowing my cover, and I won't be alone either way. Emily will be with me, and I have every intention of befriending the ghosts down there.

"I told him he could help me with my trip, and he was all in immediately." The worst thing is that, if not for the ghost issue, Gaspar would've been all in. Oh well, his loss. I'm over him. For the most part.

Gaby's relief is palpable. Her cheeks flush with colour and her shoulders relax. "Oh, that's good. I'm so... I mean, I'm glad for you!" She hugs me fiercely, soaking up my fake excitement. "I knew he would come around. You two are made for each other."

The air I breathe stabs my lungs. "Yes. It would seem that way." Okay, maybe I'm not over him. I really thought that we had something special.

"Good. Do you still want me to come, anyway? Or should I leave you two lovebirds to it?"

Even with the out, she still won't just abandon her promise. I grab her shoulders and look her in the eye. "You're off the hook. Gaspar and I've got this."

She lets out a momentous sigh, smiling weakly afterwards. "Thank god."

It's that relief that helps me keep the charade going despite my insides turning to liquid fire and a scream building in my lungs all day long.

After kissing her goodbye, I feel utterly wretched. But it had to be done. I can't risk Gaby getting hurt. And if that means tormenting myself with notions of Gaspar stepping up in her place, so be it.

Tonight, I'm going back into the catacombs with no one but Malou and the ghosts only I can see.

# CHAPTER 22

Though I still feel bad about lying to Gaby, a weight is lifted from my shoulders. I should be scared about being all alone in the catacombs, a place you shouldn't enter alone until you've had years of experience, but instead, I feel free. Even around Gaby, I uphold a mask. She's on board with the ghosts, but it's still weird, being all one-sided and such.

Down here, it doesn't matter that I talk to someone no one else can see. I don't have to constantly look over my shoulder and make sure I'm acting normal enough. I can just... be me.

Emily really knows her stuff. Just like Gaspar, she moves through the maze of tunnels without wavering, but her knowledge extends far beyond the Crossroad of the Dead, which we avoid by literally crawling through some tunnels. Malou is delighted to have me on the ground with her.

Gaby would've freaked, but once I get over the way the stone presses in on me on all sides, it's exhilarating. I feel strangely accomplished for making it through each of the narrow sections.

"You're a bona fide cataphile," Emily says after I pull myself through a window headfirst and manage not to break my neck by doing half a handstand.

I push myself up and dust off my clothes, then grab the backpack from the floor and shoulder it. "How did you get started?" I readjust Malou's leash and set her back on the ground. My hedgehog is acclimatising herself with the local fauna, trying some new bugs I barely even notice in the sparse light.

"How most people do. They hear from a friend of a friend who's been down here, ask around, and find themselves invited on a late-night stroll. I was hooked instantly. The narrow passageways, the shared secret under the city, the hidden rooms." She places her hands on her hips and glances around. "That was before I knew about the ghosts."

We've dropped into one of the big avenues that run from southwest to northeast, and ghosts are passing in front of us, barely giving us a glance.

"The ghosts are the best part of it," I claim. I have to hold it in so I won't accost these innocent bystanders and ask them all about their lives, but the older their fashion, the harder it gets.

Emily winces. "I don't know, it just feels weird. One thing that drew me to the catacombs was the solitude. This is..." She raises

192

her hand and lets it fall again. "You might as well take a walk on the Champs-Élysées."

"With fewer fuel exhausts and risk of getting run over." I have taken very few relaxing walks on the Champs-Élysées so far. "Have you met any other ghosts yet?"

"It's hard not to. Especially down here." She sounds disgruntled.

"I meant did you make friends?"

"I don't make friends easily."

My heart goes out to her. "I find it hard, too. Or at least, with the living. Ghosts are so much easier."

Emily snorts at that. "Just because you're special." She sets off walking.

"What do you mean?" I ask, hurrying after her. Malou protests a little, probably complaining about a catch slipping through her paws.

"As far as I'm concerned, dead people are the same as living people. They don't magically become open-minded or inviting just because they're dead." She sneers at a passing gentleman, who turns up his nose at her dirty clothes. "Once an asshole, always an asshole."

With a glance over her shoulder at me, she continues, "But you are different. You're an anchor to the world of the living. They flock to you because you can give them things they can no longer do for themselves. Even by just talking to them, you make them feel alive."

"Am I making you feel alive?" I ask, my mood slightly subdued. I don't like this psychoanalysis, which is threatening to taint the most enchanting part of my life.

Emily gives me another snort. "If anything, you make me feel dead."

"Oh."

"Don't take it personally, sweetie, but you're alive and I'm not. I get why all these ghosts are down here instead of up there. It's much easier to ignore you're dead without the constant reminder."

I mumble a "sorry" and drag my feet. Emily's dour attitude is a huge buzzkill. I can see why she never truly fit in, though that's a terrible thought to have. I should know, since I don't fit in either.

As we continue on our way, I keep observing the other ghosts and marvelling at our surroundings. In the beginning, there was a lot of graffiti on the wall. Some of it was done with taste, others were just tags and crude images, going against the whole idea of preserving the catacombs. The deeper we go, the fewer modern alterations we come across, but there are still pockets of surprises.

Like the room we duck into now, which has a low-hanging ceiling covered in crystals that most definitely didn't grow there.

"Lie on your back and turn off the light," Emily instructs me.

I'm all up for a break and do as I'm told. I place the backpack next to me and Malou on my stomach, then turn off the light.

At first, the darkness is oppressive. It wraps around me like a weighted blanket, crawling into my ears and my lungs. It is so complete that I realise light is the single most important thing you need to bring down here.

But then my eyes adjust. Like the first star in the night sky, one of the crystals appears in my vision. Faint, barely visible. Then another, and another, until the entire ceiling is blooming with dots of light.

My breath catches in my throat as I stare in awe. Someone put those crystals up there, placing them in a haphazard pattern to create this tapestry of light. They must have been treated with fluorescent paint, or perhaps it's a natural quality of the minerals. Whatever it is, it's beautiful. Like the neon stars my sisters and I used to have on the ceiling as children.

Unfortunately, the effect isn't to last. It needs the initial recharge of my artificial light hitting them. So after a second round of gazing at the ceiling, I have a snack and give Malou a quick belly rub before we hit the road again.

"Be careful where you place your feet," Emily calls out. "There have been a few collapses. I don't want you to fall into a hole."

Dread washes over me and I pick up Malou, while keeping my light trained on the ground. Sure enough, there are some dark patches on the path, some of which I need to climb over to avoid stepping into them. For one particularly black one, I kick a pebble into the abyss. If there is a bottom to it, I can't hear it.

"How deep are the catacombs?" I know the official data, but some depths are unexplored.

Emily just shrugs. "Who cares? Never found a way down there, so I suppose if you fall, that's it."

"Nice." What a comforting sound.

"So, this Boutique of Psychosis," I start when we're back in a more stable tunnel. "Do you know the place?" We're not planning on going there, since we don't need to get the chevalier involved.

"No." Another clipped answer, and for a moment, I'm sure it's all I'll get, but after a while, Emily turns around. "I've heard of it."

I wait for her to say more. It doesn't happen. "What did you hear?" I ask in a pained voice at last.

"Stories." She sighs heavily. "Fine, I'll tell you. If you promise not to freak."

With a title like that, I'm already anticipating a less than savoury experience. "I can handle it."

She snorts but indulges me, nevertheless. "Twenty years ago, or thereabouts, a group of cataphiles explored that area. They stayed in the boutique, which was just a nameless room back then. They were dabbling with rituals. Stupid games, nothing real. Only, when they all went to sleep, the room gave them nightmares. They woke up screaming, each of them suffering from a different psychosis. One believed a thousand ants were crawling across her skin. The other was drowning on dry land, refusing to breathe properly. And yet another was adamant he'd been buried alive. He never made it back up."

I shudder at the thought. Emily is clearly enjoying the retelling, making me think it's just one of those spooky stories people love telling.

"None of them ever recovered. It drove them all insane in a different way. That's why we call it the Boutique of Psychosis. Pick your crazy, grab a bargain." She winces at her own crude words.

"So, you've never stayed the night?"

"I never set a foot in there. Look, Alix. The catacombs are full of dark tales. We respect them, don't challenge them."

While I think that's very wise, I can't quite get over what Victor said. "Apparently, the boutique is home to the ghosts of Nexus." Since we're past the crumbly patch, I set Malou back on the ground.

In front of me, Emily's shoulders shudder. "All the more reason to stay away, then."

"Why?"

From what Victor told me, Nexus is the connection between the dead and the living. It's where I'll most likely find other ghost whisperers.

She glances back at me. "You'll see." When I raise my eyebrows, she sighs. "Just trust me on this."

I don't particularly trust Emily. Her personality is abrasive at best. She's clearly just using me for my talent. She even said so herself, but I can't help feeling responsible for her in a way. Obviously, she's new to the afterlife, and as much as she wants to pretend she's a tough cookie who doesn't need anyone, we all do.

"I don't know much about Nexus, but my ghost friend said they've built this commune. The ghosts, I mean. They could help you find your footing, help you adjust."

"Which friend was that?" she asks with a sigh.

"Victor Hugo."

"That pompous old crook?" Emily snorts. "I suppose he's been around for a while."

"One hundred and forty years, if you go by ghost time."

She stops, causing me to run into her. I stumble back, making sure I don't step on Malou in the process. Emily searches my face. "Do you *want* to go to the Boutique of Psychosis?"

My breath catches in my throat, and I swallow. Her description has me screaming no, but I can't help my curiosity. "I want to find out what the chevalier's problem with the ghosts is. Why does he want it?"

Emily sighs heavily. "Why does he want anything?" She doesn't give me an answer, though, and just continues her way. After a while, she says, "We can go if you want to. It's not far from here. And I suppose, as long as you don't sleep there, you should be fine."

Yeah, I definitely won't sleep in a place rumoured to give people psychoses. According to Hélène, I'm already suffering from one as it is. But there's no harm in visiting now. Especially since I don't plan on pulling any weird rituals. "Please."

Without another comment, Emily turns around again. "Show me that map."

She pores over it for a moment, then changes our direction and leads me through a couple of twisting tunnels until we arrive in a dead end. There, she points at the bottom, where a window leads into the darkness. "The boutique is behind this wall."

I shine my light across the wall, looking for some indication that we're in the right place. The beam gets stuck on an indention filled with blue. It isn't until I practically put my nose to it that I recognise the symbol of an eye. The iris is marked by a shard of blue ceramic, painted intricately.

"Nexus, I assume?"

"Well, are you going in or not?"

I jump when a voice appears behind me. An old woman in a crisp suit looks me up and down, then regards Emily with pity. "New to this?"

"She is," I say before Emily can brush her off.

The woman raises an eyebrow. "You're obviously not." She nods towards the entrance. "Well?"

"I'm going in." Malou is very interested in the woman's shoes, but as soon as I lower myself, she scuttles over and sniffs at the gap. "Lots of ghosts?" I don't wait for a reply. Malou never gives one. "I thought so."

Together, we climb through the bottom window. Malou goes first, and I follow. Once I drag myself up again, I stare around in wonder. The boutique is an actual room with smooth walls and a staircase leading up. I wonder if it was some kind of bunker connected to a structure on top of us, but if it was, it has since been transformed. It's like I've stepped into someone's living room.

The walls are lined with shelves that are filled with books and scrolls, dusty bottles of wine and geodes. A carpet of indistinct colour covers most of the ground, giving the room a cosy feeling that's completely out of place down here. There are chairs of all sizes, most of them occupied with ghosts who are deep in conversation.

The one thing that stands out is the column in the middle of the room. It's made up completely of bones, all wedged into each other to form the structure. The centrepiece of the column is a full skeleton of charred bones that stretches from the bottom to the top. A giant of a human, whose empty eyes stare down at me. I can see why people would attempt a ritual.

"...another one?"

I avert my eyes from the creepy column and look for the speaker. It's an imposing man in long chainmail covered by a white tunic, belted at the hips, and a white coat. A big red cross identifies him as a former Templar. The top of his head is bald, but the rest of his long hair and beard are white. Despite the age he died, he looks like he can easily take me on in a fight. Especially with the mean-looking sword at his side. "A whisperer then." His voice is used to command, its strength making me stand up straight.

The room changes ever so slightly. I assume the ghosts here are used to catacomb crawlers entering their sanctuary, oblivious to all the eyes on them, and leaving again. But I'm different.

"Uhm, I am, yes. Alix Dubois." I stretch out my hand in a gesture of goodwill.

The man stares down at it over the hook of his long nose. "How charming." He looks utterly bored. "Let me guess. You want us to sign over this room to le Chevalier d'Os."

"No. He asked me to, but I'm not getting involved in that."

A smile lights up his scowl, teeth flashing. "I think it's a little late for that, Mademoiselle Dubois."

# CHAPTER 23

M y heart thumps in my chest, impossibly loud in this room of dead people. I wet my lips as I stare at the fashionable stranger in front of me. "What do you mean?"

His smile turns into an ugly smirk. "He's got his eyes on you."

I shiver at the thought of the chevalier staking any kind of claim to me. "No. I turned him down." My voice is shaky, not at all confident.

"Yeah, good luck with that." The ghost nods towards a bottle of wine on the shelf. "Pour yourself a drink."

There's surprisingly little dust on the bottle, which tells me that someone else helped themselves to it recently. Next to it is a metal goblet, which is equally clean. Is there such a thing as ghost wine? No, if so, he wouldn't need me to pour.

I could definitely use a drink, so I wash out the goblet with some water before filling it to a third. Only then do I remember where I am, and that perhaps I shouldn't drink anything in a place dealing with psychoses.

"Drink," the ghost commands me. "I don't offer to just anyone."

I glance at Emily, who has slunk to the edge of the room, as if she needs to escape the attention that's so firmly settled on me. With a weak smile, I follow the invitation and pick up the glass I'm offered. The bouquet is so strong my head reels just taking a sniff from it. "It's not poisoned, is it?"

"What use would that be?" the ghost asks me. "Your value to anyone is in being alive, not dead."

So, now I've got value. It should probably comfort me that no one wants me dead, but all my nerves are on edge. I only manage the slightest of sips.

The wine is probably the best I've ever tasted. It's not the cheap kind Gaby and I can afford, nor a more costly drop of the kind my parents get out on special occasions. This is the kind of wine that gets served in Michelin-starred restaurants at the price of hundreds per glass. Perhaps even thousands.

"So, are you going to..." I'm not even sure what I'm supposed to ask.

"Give you the tour?" The ghost laughs. "Why don't you tell us about yourself? And how you found your way here?"

Emily obviously doesn't want to be singled out, so I just keep to the bare facts. "Well, there's not much to tell. I'm Alix and I've seen ghosts for most of my life. I work at the Panthéon and occasionally do favours for all kinds of ghosts."

Something changes in his stance. He becomes more intrigued, less threatening. "You're familiar with the Panthéon ghosts?"

I don't want to brag about Victor Hugo being my best friend, so I just nod curtly.

"Jacques de Molay." At last, he stretches out his hand. "Perhaps we can come to an agreement after all."

"About what?" I ask as I tentatively pick up the hand and give it a short squeeze. Meanwhile, my brain is reeling. I'm talking to *the* Jacques de Molay, the last grandmaster of the Templars. The one who was burned at the stake for alleged devil worship and a whole lot of other bullshit reasons.

He smirks again, his eyes giving off a dangerous glint. "I've always wanted an introduction to the Panthéon."

"Why don't you just come by?" I can barely keep myself from glancing at the charred skeleton. It must be his. Did I just make a groundbreaking discovery?

Instead of answering, Jacques brings up the chevalier again. "How long have you been working with le Chevalier d'Os? If he's got someone in on the Panthéon, he's further along than I thought."

"Further along?" What am I getting myself into here? "As I said, I'm not working with him. I met him once, and he acted weird. He wanted me to—"

"Get rid of us. I know, I know."

"Why? Is he a ghost whisperer?" I still don't get what stops him from using this room. For whatever reason he would want to.

Jacques smiles darkly. "No, he leaves the dirty work to others. He probably thought we wouldn't do anything to a harmless little girl like you. What with your doe-eyed face and unimposing stature."

My instincts are screaming at me to get out, but my feet are glued to the spot. I can't move. "What will you do to me?" The real question probably is what they did to the others. And who they were.

"You've heard the stories?" He points his thumb upward and I get that he means the room.

My throat tightens. No, no, this can't be happening. Emily said you needed to sleep in here.

All of a sudden, the grandmaster leans back. "Relax. As I said, we might come to a different agreement."

I swallow heavily, barely managing to press air into my lungs. "What kind of agreement?"

"An introduction to Voltaire, Hugo, and the whole conclave up there. They don't meet with the likes of us, but you'll change that. Invoke my name once they've agreed." He doesn't leave any room for me to agree or not. "In return, our protection in the catacombs. Our protection from *him*."

"Le Chevalier d'Os?" I whisper, my words little more than a breath.

I still don't know enough about what the hell is going on here to assess my situation. Obviously, my sanity is in danger right now, but how much of a danger is le Chevalier d'Os? Is he even the one I should be wary of? What if the reason he wants these ghosts evicted is because of the danger they pose? Perhaps those claims of devil worship weren't just a front.

Gaspar talked about the cataphiles as this wholesome group of people who want to explore and preserve the catacombs. The chevalier was supposed to be some kind of leader. Perhaps he only seized the chance to make the catacombs a little safer.

But it doesn't matter what's real or not. The only thing that matters is that I get out of here with my life and my sanity intact. The price for it is suspiciously low. "I'll talk to Victor and let him know about your request."

The grandmaster smiles. "Good. I knew we could come to an agreement. Now, off you go, finish your little business and get me that meeting."

The sudden dismissal flies straight over my head. I still have so many questions.

Jacques' grin grows a little insane. "Now," he snaps.

And then I hear it. There are steps coming down the stairs. From the way the stairs vibrate, their sound echoing through the room, it can only mean one thing: someone alive is approaching.

"Don't get caught," Jacques whispers.

This time, his words hurtle me out of the room. I scrape Malou from the ground and duck below. Flickering light floods the room behind me.

"Halt!" a voice calls. "Who's there?"

I don't bother replying. Instead, I pull myself through the opening on the other side, grab my backpack, and run down the tunnel in headless panic.

Steps soon thunder down the stone behind me, multiple shouts muffled by the walls. There must be a whole group on my heels, at least. Light dances on my shoulder just before I throw myself into another tunnel. Whenever I look back, I see nothing but a glare of light. Blinded, I speed up. In my haste, I overlook a pile of rocks and land face first in the dust.

Malou squeaks and I'm worried I've hurt her, but if she's still making sounds that at least means she's alive. And so am I, despite the stabbing pain in my elbows.

The madness still has its hold on me, so I push myself up and stumble into the adjacent corridor, only to face more lights.

Like a deer in headlights, I stare a little too long when suddenly, someone grabs my elbow and tugs me to the side. I fall into their arms and they put me upright before dragging me along. Left and right we go, up some stairs and down a tunnel.

At long last, the steps and shouts are far behind us. We slow down, but I still can't think straight, my breaths impossibly loud in my ear.

"You're safe, Alix. I've got you. You're safe."

Slowly, the voice penetrates my irrational fear, and I turn my head upward. In the light of my headlamp, I see a shadowed jaw, soft dark hair, and wide brown eyes.

"Gaspar?"

# CHAPTER 24

My brain is having trouble comprehending what I'm seeing. After the indescribable panic that gripped me, my wild flight, and the confusing crumbs of information I received in the Boutique of Psychosis, the world has fallen off its wheels. Gaspar can't be down here. He never came. We broke up.

There's a growl coming from Malou's carry bag. Malou!

I stumble away from Gaspar and carefully insert my fingers into the bag to lift out Malou. She's pulled herself into a tight little ball. Oh, how I wish I could shut the world off like that. "I'm sorry, little one," I whisper and hold her close to my chest.

"Is she okay?" Gaspar asks. He's still there.

Suspiciously, I take another step away. "What are you doing here?"

He looks utterly miserable. "I found your message."

"And?" I stroke Malou, and slowly, I feel her uncurl against my chest.

"And I'm sorry. I shouldn't have flown off the handle like that." He winces at his choice of words. "You can see ghosts."

"I'm not going to defend myself." Now that Malou isn't rolled up anymore, I wriggle two fingers between us and stroke her tummy in calm, reassuring circles. "Nor do I want to fight again."

"I don't want to fight either. I'm sorry we did in the first place." He runs his fingers through his hair, still miserable. "It scared me at first, but it's all good now." When I raise my eyebrows, Gaspar sighs. "I mean, I believe you, and I'm... I'm okay with it."

Slowly, I lower myself against the wall, cradling Malou between my fingers, and close my eyes. "Are you really?"

"One hundred percent, yes."

I open one of my eyes. That's surprisingly certain for someone who ghosted me for a week after his big freak-out. "One hundred percent?"

Gaspar nods, determined. "There's no doubt about it."

Can I really trust him? My heart yearns to say yes—I could really use a friend right about now, but it seems too easy. "No doubts?"

"Well, if I had one, it's gone now. No level-one cataphile would have navigated the catacombs as easily as you did."

"How did you find out where I was going?" I never had the chance to talk to Gaspar about the Boutique of Psychosis or show him the map, and I only told him when I would enter the cata-combs again, nothing else.

Gaspar scrunches up his face. "I went back to the Crossroad of the Dead, thinking you returned to the chevalier. He told me where he sent you, but couldn't confirm you were actually heading that way."

"The chevalier." The mysterious Knight of Bones, enemy of the ghosts—or at least the enemy of some dangerous, mind-bending ghosts that held enough power to rule a state within a state when they were alive.

"Can I sit?" Gaspar nods at my side.

If I'm being honest, I could use a little human warmth. Yes, he hurt me, but he's come back. It just took him a little longer than I'd hoped.

Gaspar hunkers down next to me, then shyly raises his arm. When I nod, he puts it around my shoulders and pulls me close. We sit together in silence until my heart rate has normalised, and I feel myself easing into his body. On my chest, Malou has gone quiet too. She's probably sleeping.

"Did you go into the Boutique of Psychosis?" Gaspar asks softly.

I assume he knows the stories about the place. "Yes. And it's full of ghosts." Holding my breath, I wait for the telltale signs of disbelief. But there's no sudden tension in his body, no gasp, no withdrawing of his arm. "I believe the ghosts are the ones who make you go mad. They certainly put fear into my heart." To spur me on, I suppose.

Bit by bit, I tell Gaspar about my experience in the Boutique of Psychosis. At some point, I lower Malou into her pouch and feed her some cat food from the bag. When I get to the point of how I even got there, I notice that I've left Emily behind. I glance down the tunnel and see her waiting for me further down, keeping a respectful distance. She's not one to give up.

"So, the ghosts are part of Nexus?" Gaspar asks.

I shrug my shoulders. "That's what Victor said, and I trust him."

Gaspar huffs softly. "I can't believe that you're actually best friends with Victor Hugo. That's crazy." When I draw away a little, he quickly shakes his head. "I didn't say, you're crazy, just that it's insane—no, unbelie—I'm really bad with words. My prof would agree."

Chuckling, I lean back into him. Something as mundane as essays for class takes the fear away. "I understand what you're trying to say. I never would've thought I'd be friends with the ghosts of Victor Hugo, Voltaire, and all the others, either. But I am."

"Metal. That's what it is." He grins at me.

Heat blooms in my stomach as I see his signature smile once more turned out for me. "Thank you."

"For what?"

"For being here. And for believing in me." I open my arms and wrap them both around his body, snuggling into his side. Glancing up at him, I ask, "You're going to stay, right?"

Gaspar's lips brush my forehead. "For as long as you'll have me."

Now that all of my adrenaline has passed through my veins, I'm bone-tired. Time stands still in the catacombs. I might have been down here for two hours or ten. It honestly feels like days. My eyes are getting heavy, exhaustion setting in. "Tell me about yourself," I whisper. "Do you have siblings?"

Gaspar's voice reverberates through his chest directly into my ear, but it's more a feeling than a sound. The words he says don't register in my brain, just the timbre of his voice and the heat of his body, until I drift away completely.

# CHAPTER 25

I wake up curled in Gaspar's lap, his hand on my head, fingers tangled in my hair.

He's already awake. "First night in the catacombs, huh?"

My body hurts from the hard ground and cramped pose I fell asleep in. Surprisingly, I'm not cold, though. The temperature never really changed that much. Neither did the darkness. "Is it night?"

"Probably not," Gaspar admits.

I check the time on my phone. Since I haven't used it at all down here, it still has plenty of battery. It's 14:17. We're in the middle of the afternoon. When did I fall asleep last night? My sense of time is completely skewed.

"Time doesn't exist down here," Gaspar muses with a half-smile. "It's all one to me either way."

"Way to be dramatic." I sit up and stretch, then grab some of the food in my backpack. "Do you need something?"

"I'm okay."

I feel a bit self-conscious eating in front of him, but I'm starving. It's a simple meal, just some bread, cheese, and dried fruit washed down with water. And with no one else eating, I make quick progress of it.

"So, what's next?" Gaspar asks.

"We go to Ossa Arida," Emily says, her voice impatient. I suppose it was boring to watch us sleep all night... day.

"I think we can both agree that we want nothing to do with Nexus or anyone else down here."

Gaspar nods. "That all sounds messed up, agreed."

"So, we go to Ossa Arida. Emily, that's the ghost, will lead us off the map. She's over there." I point to her for Gaspar's benefit, and he does a passable job of looking in her direction. "How far do we have to go?"

"Not far, but it's not an easy path."

I shoulder my backpack and make sure Malou is secured. "All right. We've come this far. We can get further."

Emily gives me a sharp nod and starts leading us down the corridor.

We don't talk a lot. Emily seems extra stoic today, and Gaspar is too nervous to question anything that's happening. He's staying by my side, though, and for that, I'm grateful. I'm still a bit sore about what happened at the Seine, but the more time we spend in each other's vicinity, the easier we slip back into our initial easy companionship.

"Have you ever been here?" I ask, my whisper travelling unnaturally loud through the tunnel.

From ahead, Emily hushes me, while Gaspar shakes his head. "I have no idea where we are," he admits.

A chilling thought, for sure. I notice that there are no street signs in these tunnels, nor any other helpful installations to orient yourself, but Emily never steers from her path.

The tunnel is slowly getting wetter, our steps squelching below us, then our feet are sloshing through water. For a place called dry bones, it's certainly a wet approach.

The water keeps rising, while the ceiling is lowering. Soon, we have to drop on all fours to continue, dragging our bodies through the water. I make sure that Malou's pouch rests securely on top of my upper back and follow Emily's lead.

"How did you find out about this place?" Never in a million years would I have come up with the idea of trying out this flooded, narrow tunnel to see where it leads.

"I just did." Emily's reply is as frustrating as always.

Behind me, Gaspar also responds to me. "We all explore a little, I suppose. I mean, if it's a tunnel, they usually lead somewhere."

"Unless there's a cave-in," Emily mutters.

I whimper, for a moment losing the hold on my precious sanity. For the most part, I'm able to ignore the weight of my surroundings. But there are tons of rock above me and on top of that, a city. Cars, buildings, millions of people.

"You've got this." Gaspar's voice anchors me in the here and now, and I manage to drag myself on.

The going is tough. Before, the narrow passages always lasted only a short time, but this one keeps dragging on. My muscles are cramping, especially the ones in my neck, since I have to hold up my head to keep my face out of the water. I don't dare think about having to backtrack. Instead, I keep telling myself that the end is near in fifteen more seconds. Then another fifteen and another.

It's a lot of fifteen seconds when the ceiling finally slopes up again. The water stays with us for a while longer, but at least we can walk through it now instead of crawling.

A set of stairs leads us into a narrow room with a well. "Is this it?" I ask, hopeful.

"Almost," Emily breathes, then puts her finger on her mouth. She moves through a wall, leaving us behind.

From what I can see, the room doesn't have an exit. I really hope Emily doesn't expect me to pass through the wall like she did, because that means I've completely wasted my time.

She returns a little later. "The path is clear. Come on."

"Em—"

Instead of passing through the wall again, she moves towards the well. "You need to climb down here. Use your hands and feet to hold onto the sides. I promise it's not deep."

Her promise doesn't fill me with confidence. Apart from the manhole entrances, I've never considered a vertical descent within the catacombs. My muscles feel too weak after the ordeal they just went through, so I nibble on a piece of salami first before I attempt another strenuous exercise.

"Do you trust her?" Gaspar asks, sounding just as exasperated as I feel.

"Let's just get it done." It's safe to say I don't want to work for Emily ever again. This medallion is nothing but trouble, in my opinion. I can't wait to hand it off to her daughter and wash my hands of the catacombs.

Gaspar insists on climbing in first to catch me in case I slip. I have no idea what to expect from this kind of climbing. Once I've pushed my hands and feet into the walls of the well, though, it's surprisingly easy. The walls are made of compacted soil and there are embedded pebbles for me to hold onto. It makes them less slippery. As long as I keep my limbs stretched, I feel pretty secure.

That is, until my light washes over the pebbles. It's not gravel I'm holding onto. It's knobs of bones.

Ossa Arida. Dry bones. Of course, there would be bones.

I manage to keep my freak-out contained until my feet touch the ground. Under the weight of my shoes, more bones splinter, and I wince. I've just pulverised someone's remains.

"They're long dead," Gaspar whispers, holding me in the darkness.

"No ghosts around," I confirm. These bones are leftovers from the big move, their souls long moved on. "Is this it?" I ask impatiently, not relishing the idea of having to search for the medallion among the bones.

"She went through there," Gaspar explains, pointing to an opening at the bottom of the well. Not the end, then. "It's really narrow. You'll have to hook your backpack around your feet and put your arms above your head, then pull yourself through. There's a bend, so don't panic when you hit it."

I want to know where he got that information from, but my throat is too tight to ask. Not for the first time, I ask myself what I got myself into.

As if in a trance, I lower myself, using my hands to test the opening. It feels impossibly small. Am I really going to fit through this? As Gaspar said, I take off my backpack and put Malou inside, so I won't squash her. Then I loop the handles around my feet and try pulling it. It's not easy, but it works. At last, I extend my arms above my head and dive into the hole like a swimmer.

My breath sticks in my chest as the soil and bones press against my body. The tunnel is so small I can't lower my arms. There's only forward. It's okay for the first bit, but once I've pulled my whole body in, panic seizes me. I'm lying flat in a tube of bones, my movements severely constricted. My backpack blocks the path behind me, its bulky mass a pain to pull through just with my feet.

I can't move. Forth or back, it doesn't matter.

Seconds pass and sweat trickles down my face, my breathing flat. Will my bones be the next ones added to Ossa Arida?

No, I won't simply give up and lie here until death comes for me. I manage to fight down the panic and reach further with my arms. My fingertips find purchase on the bones, and I manage to drag myself forward another few inches.

That's right. Just continue bit by bit.

It feels counter-intuitive to keep going forwards instead of escaping the tunnel, but I'm already committed to the movement when that thought enters my mind, so I keep going.

A few more inches and then my hands find only a wall. My heart jumps into my throat. The sweat on my face stinks sour.

The bend. Gaspar warned me about a bend.

I feel around with my hands and manage to locate the direction of the bend. My body doesn't bend that way, so I slowly twist onto my back. My knees scrape over the tunnel walls. I feel soil trickling on my face as I find purchase on a thighbone. Ignoring the pains in my body and the oppressive feel of the walls, I pull my body up.

When I search for a continuation of the path, my fingers suddenly grab an edge. A rim! There's an end to this tunnel.

I keep wriggling my body forward and upward until first my hands and at long last my elbows are in the open. Using my arms as levers, I push myself further. My body is now folded in half around the bend, but my head is in the open. I can breathe.

It takes me another minute to get the rest of my body out of the hole. The backpack gets stuck on the bend, but with Gaspar pushing from behind and a bit of wriggling, I manage to get it out.

Suddenly, I slip. My bum hits the ground. More bones are squashed, their splinters driven into my left hand. My right hand has landed on something soft and squishy.

I hold my breath in fear as I slowly turn around. The light washes over walls of bone. The floor is covered just the same. But there's something bulky on the ground. Something big. Something covered in sticky blood.

The scream tears from my throat the moment I realise what I'm looking at.

# CHAPTER 26

There's a dead body in this room. I drop out of the hole and scramble as far away as I possibly can before my back hits a wall. Bones splinter under my weight, adding to the unspeakable fear that has taken hold of me.

My light dances through the room ahead of me, sometimes showing the body, sometimes just the bones of those who came before it. Through the glimpses it shows me, I take note of some of its features.

Long green hair, thigh-length waders, empty eyes, blood on the face.

The face!

I know that face.

Another scream escapes me. Or perhaps I've never stopped screaming.

Then suddenly, Gaspar is there. He gathers me in his arms, pressing his hands on my head as he pulls me into his chest. "I'm here. I'm here."

The screams break off, and I start sobbing uncontrollably. I'm a complete mess, and it's all Emily's fault.

"You didn't tell me!" I shout at the ghost standing on the other side of the room, looking down at her dead body with dispassion.

"What?" Gaspar asks softly. He's stroking my back and keeps holding me close. "What should I have told you?"

I push him away. Not because he deserves it, but because I need room to breathe. "Not you—her!"

"You wouldn't have come for me," Emily says in a matter-of-fact voice.

"What do you mean?" Understanding blooms on my tongue. "Oh. Oh, no." Shuddering, I close my eyes, but the sight of her dead body is imprinted on my mind and I can't find reprieve. "There's no medallion, right? Is there even a daughter?"

Emily pushes off the opposite wall, pulling up her shoulders. "There is, but she lives with her dad. We don't talk much."

A whimper escapes me. "The thing you lost was your body. You wanted me to find your body."

"It's important."

"It's fucked up!"

The last thing I need after the ordeal of getting here is a visual reminder that people *do* die in the catacombs. "What were you expecting me to do with it?"

There's no way I can carry this body with me on my way back up. Not even with Gaspar's help. We wouldn't even be able to get it through the tunnel we just came through.

"Lead the police to it."

Yeah, the police will not follow me all this way into the catacombs.

My mind is still jumping all over the place. I force myself to breathe through my nose, push the fact that there's a dead body mere inches from me away, and try to think through what little I can do.

"They need to know I was murdered."

I jerk up my head. "You were murdered?"

As if it wasn't bad enough that she died in this place, now she's telling me that she was killed down here?

I glance at the body, for the first time taking a good look at it. Emily is right. She was murdered. There's no way the bloody wound on her forehead has come from a fall. "You were shot."

"Yes."

"By whom?"

Emily's jaw hardens. "Le Chevalier d'Os."

My heart stops. I see him before me: his accurate haircut, his dark eyes, his grip around my wrist. Emily telling me to run.

"I met a murderer?" My voice is a shaky whisper, unable to hold on to the words.

"I'm so sorry," Gaspar whispers next to me, equally shaken. He obviously had no idea what sinister things were going on down here. "I have no words."

Desperately, I search for his hand, squeezing it tight when I find it. "It's all my fault." I suddenly feel so stupid. Everything Hélène had said about me was true. I constantly get myself into danger and for what? The catacombs are dangerous, and it goes far beyond endless darkness and confusing corridors.

"Well, you're here now," Emily says. "Might as well do what we came for and leave."

If she weren't already dead, I would murder her. "What did we come for?" I ask because I have no idea what I'm supposed to do now. "I came for some lost property, not this."

Emily waves me off. "You're welcome to take whatever is left as long as you take some pictures, so the police know what's happened down here."

"What *did* happen?" Despite myself, I manage to pull myself up and grasp my phone. Her suggestion isn't that bad after all. I can take photos.

My hands shake though, and the light conditions are bad, so I've no idea how useful these pictures will be to anyone.

"I picked up rumours of someone doing rituals down here. We don't want any satanists in the catacombs," Emily explains, not caring about what these words do to me. So, now the chevalier is a satanist. "There was a lot of that in the eighties, but the cataphiles cleaned up. If we find someone pulling that kind of shit, we tell the cataflics. The catacombs are for exploration and art, not such bullshit.

"So, I followed the rumours, and I came across Ossa Arida." She points upwards, and for the first time, I notice that there's a second room above us. A staircase in a corner leads up to the second level.

Emily encourages me to take a look, and Gaspar and I leave her dead body behind to climb up. What we see up here chills me even further.

Someone has built an altar from a huge round stone table. Instantly, my eyes are drawn to the engraved pentagram, and the bones laid out like the Vitruvian Man between its points. Unlit black candles are placed at each line crossing and tip of the pentagram. Dried herbs are crumpled all across the body.

Though it looks as if we interrupted the ritual, no one else is here, not even the ghost of this unfortunate soul. "What's happening here?" I whisper.

Gaspar grasps me, his fingers digging into my hip. "I don't know, but we've got to leave."

I don't want to squeeze through the hole again—or climb the well and crawl through water—but he's right. We've obviously stumbled onto something sinister. Sinister enough to be murdered for it.

I snap a quick picture before running back down to Emily's body. There, I grab my backpack and hook it back onto my feet. This time, I have to crawl into the cavity upside down and on my back. It takes a couple of tries, but with Gaspar's help, I manage. Knowing what to expect and how long it will take helps with not losing my head this time.

Gaspar and I climb the well and then start our long crawl back through the water. I'm tired to the bone by the time the water shallows, and we come out the other side.

"Told you we had mice. Very wet mice."

A light is blinding me. Before I can make out the speaker in the brightness, I catch a glimpse of something else.

A gun.

# CHAPTER 27

"Alix!" Gaspar grabs my hand and propels me forward. I bump into the woman with the gun and hear it falling from her hand. The second person tries to grab me, but the surprise is on our side, and I slip free.

Our steps thunder down the corridors, my light flashing wildly across the walls. Behind us, shouts arise. "Get the ghost whisperer!"

That's the chevalier's voice. The one who murdered Emily.

Speaking of Emily, she's nowhere to be seen. Which means Gaspar and I are running blind. It doesn't matter. We have to get away before we can worry about getting lost.

"Lose the backpack!" Gaspar shouts at me.

He helps me out of the straps. I grab Malou and sling her carry bag across my shoulder before dropping the pack. Hopefully, our pursuers will stumble and roll an ankle.

It doesn't happen. Their lights keep chasing us down the tunnels. I'm faster without the backpack, but I'm also exhausted. Adrenaline or not, my body isn't able to uphold this pace for long.

"Alix, here!" Gaspar points at something on the ground.

I would have almost stumbled into a dark hole. Glad that Gaspar pointed it out, I attempt to step across it, but he shakes his head. "Down, quick."

I stare at him with wide eyes, the steps of our pursuers behind us. Gaspar doesn't wait. He grabs my wrists and pushes me sideways. My feet lose their grip on the ground, and I fall.

Darkness.

The fall snatches the light from me. Or maybe Gaspar did. It doesn't last long. I hit a pile of rocks and half roll, half skitter down until my feet hit the mud and my body comes to a rest. Above me, Gaspar keeps running ahead. A few seconds later, more steps can be heard. They barely stop to go past the hole before resuming their run. Soon, the faint glimmer of their light vanishes, and I'm alone in the darkness.

My brain is still catching up with what has happened when I hear the sound of a shot. The shock reverberates through the tunnel and into my bones.

I sit still, my brain lost to the terror. Gaspar isn't here. Gaspar has run on, drawing them away from the hole. Drawing them away from me.

There was a shot.

I taste bile in my throat, and then I'm shaking. "No," I whisper. This can't be happening. Gaspar did not just get shot. He's alive. The shot didn't hit him.

But there is no second shot. No second attempt.

A sob tears itself from my throat. I clamp my hands across my mouth to keep the sound in. If Gaspar was shot, they might come back to me. I need to move so his sacrifice wasn't in vain.

I have no idea how I manage to drag myself up. With my hands, I feel around the cavity, making sure I also run them across the ceiling to avoid a sudden impact. Slowly, I set my feet in a direction. One step in front of the other.

Tears are streaming down my face, the stale air doing nothing to ease my pain.

It's not until ten minutes later that I remember I'm not completely without light. The headlamp is gone, and so is everything in my backpack, but I've still got my phone.

"Please be gone," I whisper to myself as I manage to unlock the phone and turn on the light. I keep it on the lowest setting, which still gives me plenty of light to look around.

I'm on a lower level inside a reasonably wide corridor. There are no street signs to guide me. I have no idea where I am or which direction I'm going, but I keep trudging on, driven by a fear larger than the catacombs.

It's not until I get to a crossing that I break down. What am I doing here? Should I go back for Gaspar? Will I be shot next? I hate

Emily with a passion. Sure, she didn't plan on getting murdered either, but she chose to hide this very important fact from me. I do little favours for ghosts. I don't investigate their deaths.

And now Gaspar might be dead because of her.

No! I shake my head. I can't allow myself to believe that. Gaspar has to have escaped. He knows the catacombs. He knows how to escape. Which is much more than can be said for me.

I know that I'm in deep shit now. All I've got left is a phone with decreasing battery power and Malou.

Malou. I need my pet hedgehog now.

Fortunately, our escape hasn't hurt her in any way. I dig my fingers into the soft fur of her belly and calm myself by rubbing circles into it. Malou enjoys the attention, oblivious to our impending doom. Oh god, Malou's stuck down here with me. Why did I take her?

I remind myself that she's a hedgehog, guided by smell more than sight and there are bugs down here, so hopefully, she will cope. I just have to let her go.

My hands shake. I don't want to be all alone. But she's an innocent. The least I can do after dragging her down here is give her a chance.

"You'll find the way out, right?" I put Malou on the ground and run my shaking fingers across her spikes.

Malou looks at me, but she doesn't like the light, so she turns away again. Snuffling loudly, she starts off into the darkness. I follow her, unable to part with her just yet.

The path meets some stairs and I lift her up since she seems determined to go this way. As we slowly climb higher, the walls start shaking. A deep rumble sounds right next to me. "What..."

The Métro. There are no earthquakes in Paris, but the Métro runs deep. If it can make the walls around me shake, that means I must be close to one of the tunnels.

Hope blooms in my chest, my heart rate accelerating. I shed the exhaustion and keep following the tunnel into the darkness.

A second rumble occurs, and it feels like the Métro is going right over my head. As scary as the thought is, it spurs me on to keep going. Please let there be a connection somewhere. There has to be, right?

If so, Malou will find it. I let her down again, even though there is no other way to go. Malou continues on the hunt for an exit, and we bustle through the tunnel together.

At last, there's an intersection ahead of us. I glance to the right when I pick up the faintest of drafts going through my hair. I turn to the left and scream.

There's a man ahead of me. My phone falls to the ground, and I jump away, but the man manages to grasp my wrist.

"Don't!" he says. It's not particularly threatening, more like a warning.

My overwrought brain can't cope with it. I thrash in his grip, desperate to get away. Whether a ghost or one of the chevalier's people or someone from Nexus, I only know I need to run.

Unfortunately, he knows exactly what he's doing. "Calm down. I'm not going to hurt you." He fumbles out a card. "Police. I'm police."

"Police?" I blurt out. That's another group I've been running from today. "You're real. Alive and…" What am I saying there? Of course, he's alive.

The man smiles faintly. "I'm not a ghost, that's right. But you look like you've seen several."

I swallow heavily. "I haven't. I mean, that's not…" Reality slams back into me, my brain picking up its normal functions. "Oh, you need to come with me. My friend is still in there. He might be hurt. Shot."

The police officer's eyebrows crawl up. He nods over my shoulder, then asks. "Shot?" Then he looks me up and down. "Is this all you came down with here?"

My knees are weak as I shake my head. "No. I had a backpack and Gaspar. Gaspar du Charbonneau. We…" I have to take a deep breath, the story threatening to spill out of me incoherently. "We came down here after a tip. A rotten tip. We found a dead body and a ritual place." Emily had said that the police wants to know about that. "When we tried to leave, we were accosted by two people.

They had guns. Gaspar pushed me down a hole and drew them away. I heard a shot."

My voice gives way. Fresh tears roll down my face.

"You said his name was Gaspar du Charbonneau?" the policeman asks to confirm.

I nod, then describe him as best as I can. "Please. You've got to find him."

He doesn't run off, though. Instead, he bends down and picks up my phone. "I hate doing this, but you've got enough battery power to keep going. So listen well." He points down the corridor he's come from. "You walk this way for about ten minutes. There will be a set of stairs on your left. Go up, take the right path. You should reach a door. I want you to *wait* for me in the Métro station."

"There is a Métro station?"

"Can you remember that?" When I nod, he puts the phone in my hand. "What's your name?"

"Alix Dubois." I don't care if I get in trouble. There's a fine for entering the catacombs, but I'll gladly pay it if I get Gaspar back safely.

With a last, "Remember to wait for me," he leaves me on my own and heads down the path I came from.

As it turns out, Malou knows exactly where to go. I catch up with her at the stairs. By stretching her little body, she's already made it up two steps.

I pick her up and nuzzle my nose into her belly fur. "You're such a clever girl."

Together, we climb the rest of the stairs. The draft is undeniable here, and we soon arrive at the door. It's a heavy one, but with my last strength, I manage to pull it open enough to squeeze out. A glaring "No Entry" sign is screwed to the other side of it.

Fluorescent light floods my senses. I blink hastily, my eyes tearing from the overstimulation. I'm in one of the abandoned Métro stations that are filled with graffiti from bottom to top. There's not another soul down here, but I notice a camera filming the corner I emerged from.

I've made it. I escaped the catacombs with my life and body intact.

But Emily was murdered.

And Gaspar might be dead.

Sobbing, I sink to the ground.

# CHAPTER 28

The wait is excruciating. I fluctuate between inconsolable sobbing and agitated walking around. When the temptation to go back into the catacombs becomes too much, I text Gaby.

My phone goes dead before she arrives, but there's an old clock in the Métro station that tells me we're going on eleven p.m. It's been over twenty-four hours since I stepped into the city under our feet, unaware of how much it would mess me up. Or what it would cost me.

"Alix!" Gaby comes down the stairs, looking confused.

As soon as I see my best friend, I'm up and throwing myself into her arms. "Gaspar might be dead."

"What?" Even confused, Gaby knows what to do. She hugs me fiercely. "What happened? Why are you here?"

"I need to wait," I whine, then tell her the whole story in chopped bits that probably make no sense at all. "They fired a gun. Emily died by gunshot. They murdered her and now they... they..." Sobs ravage my throat. I can't imagine how I'll live with myself, knowing that Gaspar died because of my insistence on helping every ghost I come across.

Gaby strokes my hair and keeps holding me close. She leads me to the stairs and sits me down, then proceeds to check me all over. I've been out here for almost two hours, but I have yet to take stock of myself. It's only when Gaby runs her fingers over my hands that I notice how many cuts and scrapes they sustained. My fingernails are all torn and bloody.

"Can you hurt a ghost? Because I want to beat that Emily woman up big time."

I've got hiccups from crying so much. "She was murdered, Gaby."

"Yes, but she had no right to involve you. She certainly didn't have the right to do so under false premises." Gaby huffs angrily. "She only cared about herself. I'm sorry to say it, but you were only a tool for her to use."

Emily never pretended otherwise. She outright told me that ghosts only come to me because they want something from me. "I'm done with ghosts," I whisper.

"Are you?" Gaby asks, not sounding convinced.

"Well, I'll stick with Victor. But no more favours. And certainly no more catacombs."

Gaby hugs me fiercely again. "Yes, please. Never ever go down there again. The ghosts and cataphiles deserve each other. They don't deserve you."

It's another hour until the door opens, and the policeman emerges. He's surprisingly young, probably no more than three years older than me. His blond hair is closely cropped, his face clean-shaven. He's wearing a black pullover under an equally black bullet-proof vest and dark cargo pants. And he's carrying a concealed weapon.

I swallow heavily at the sight of the gun. But the worst thing is that he came out alone. Gaspar isn't with him. He does have my backpack, though.

He raises an eyebrow at Gaby but nods thoughtfully. "I'm glad you're still here. I went back the way you said. Found your backpack, but no trace of your friend or anyone else. You've been lucky to get lost so close to this exit." He drops the backpack at my feet. "You look like shit, so I'm not gonna bother with the fine. Just want to remind you that it is illegal to enter the catacombs. For good reason. As you've hopefully learnt today."

"Her boyfriend might have been murdered, and you're lecturing her on trespassing?" Gaby asks. "Shouldn't you be calling for back up and launching an investigation or something?"

He nods thoughtfully. "I will transfer the case to the local department, but they usually don't take catacomb matters very far. By the time the police get down there, they'll have everything moved. Especially because you escaped." He smiles weakly. "Which is a good thing."

I'm confused. "I thought you were police."

"Special ops." He takes a moment to think through what he's about to say next, his forehead wrinkling. "Listen, your friend..."

"He might still be alive, right?" Gaby asks. "He's a cataphile. That means he's probably found a different exit by now."

The police officer frowns. "You're a friend of Gaspar's as well?"

"Not yet," Gaby admits. "But I will be when Alix introduces us. They only got together recently."

Once again, the man gives me a thoughtful glance. "I see. Well, I need to ask you a couple of questions. Alone, preferably."

Gaby's arms around me tighten. "No way. Can't you see she's been through enough? Alix needs rest, and she needs her boyfriend to be alive." For some reason, the policeman winces at that. "Will questioning her right now help with the latter?"

"We can do this when you've recovered a little," he concedes, to my surprise. "But we *will* have to talk."

Dread settles over me. I know that I can't get around questioning after the tale I've already spun for him. I'll either have to lie or tell him about the ghosts. Both seem like recipes for disaster to me. Nevertheless, I hand over my details and promise once more not to set another foot into the catacombs. He offers to drive us home.

"Try to get some sleep." Once again, he looks like he wants to say more, but he keeps his promise to Gaby and leaves it at giving me his card. "Call me when you're ready."

*Sébastien Roubert, GoPol Paris.*

I stuff the card into my pocket and follow Gaby upstairs into her flat. She barely manages to get some food into me and my skin washed before I fall into her bed, too exhausted to move another limb or shed another tear. But sleep won't come to me, and so Gaby tells me that Gaspar will be fine over and over again. How I'll see him Monday at Sorbonne. Or how he'll call as soon as he's made it back to the surface.

By the time I finally fall asleep, I almost believe it.

# CHAPTER 29

Sunday is the worst. I feel all the aches in my body and the deeper one in my heart. Gaspar does not call, nor does he answer his phone. I'm worried sick. I can't stop seeing Emily's dead body or the pentagram with its bones. And I hear at least five gunshots, or what I think might be gunshots at first. I keep expecting le Chevalier d'Os to turn up on my doorstep, and keep reminding myself that he doesn't know where I live.

To distract me, Gaby and I focus on piecing together all the things I stumbled on in the catacombs, trying to make sense of what I've seen. Gaby even started making a vision board.

"So, Nexus is an informal organisation concerned with creating a commune down in the catacombs. They're made up of ghosts and the living alike, led by *the* freaking Jacques de Molay." Gaby points at the middle of her board, while I sit on the bed with

Malou on my lap. "And their headquarters sit in the Boutique of Psychosis.

"Now, since the Chevalier d'Os wanted to get rid of the ghosts, we can safely assume that he's *not* a part of Nexus. Instead, he's some sort of satanist, doing sinister rituals in the catacombs." Until now, I've been unable to separate the two, but Gaby is right. Gaspar worked on the assumption the chevalier was involved with Nexus, but that's highly unlikely. "What did they say?"

I try to recall the exact words. "That he was further along than they thought."

"Because he sent you to them?"

"Molay thought I worked for him and… the Panthéon. He thought he had an in with Victor and the others, which wasn't true, so instead *he* wants an in now." I still have to tell Victor about my adventure, and Jacques de Molay wants me to introduce them to each other. All I can do is suggest it to Victor. It'll be the last favour I'll do, since I can't really see the harm in it and promised them. After that, I want nothing more to do with any of the catacomb ghosts.

Gaby frowns. "What's stopping him from just talking to the Panthéon ghosts themselves? Emily just waltzed in without a problem."

"Not into the crypt." I frown, trying to remember the details of our two meetings. "She always appeared upstairs, and Victor was prepared to throw her out. He also wanted me to stay away from the catacombs. Said he's not interested in what Nexus proposes. Not his vibe."

"He did not say vibe."

I giggle, though the sound is all wrong after what potentially happened to Gaspar. "He did."

"Huh." Gaby puts the Panthéon on her vision board as a third group. "So, the Panthéon wants nothing to do with the catacombs, but the catacombs want everything to do with the Panthéon. Nexus does, and they assumed the chevalier had succeeded where they didn't, so he must want it too."

"But why?" I run my hands over my face, too tired to think.

Gaby leaves her vision board and climbs onto the bed to hug me. "I don't know. Sorry, we should probably leave it alone. This is obviously a ghost matter, and we're done with that."

I nod shakily. That's right, my time as a ghost whisperer has officially come to an end. Hélène will be delighted to hear it. I'm not kidding myself. I will still see ghosts, and I won't forsake my friendships at the Panthéon, but that will be the extent of it. No more favours that get me or others into trouble. The ghosts will have to sort themselves out or just give up on mortal matters.

But damn, it's intriguing how involved they still are beyond death. No one can say that the afterlife is in any way boring.

"You know. I never found anyone like me down there," I muse, suddenly reminded of my original motivation.

Gaby takes a deep breath and shrugs. "It's probably for the better. If they hang out with le Chevalier d'Os, you don't want to be friends with them."

I lean against her shoulder. "You're right. You're always right."

If only I had listened to her in the first place.

Monday marks the second day without notice from Gaspar. I'm physically sick throughout my lectures and don't retain a single thing. I keep looking out for Gaspar's floppy hair among the students on campus, but while his style is not exactly unique, none of the people I see are him.

Finally, I return to the library and find the book on catacombs. My note is still stuck in there, no other message in sight. With a heavy sigh, I cast around the long benches.

This time, my gaze falls on a guy with a familiar band shirt. It's not Gaspar—his hair blond and shoulder-length—but he's into the same obscure music. I tell myself it's worth a try to make my way over.

"Hi." I wave shyly when I reach his place at the bench.

The guy startles and takes a headphone out, looking askance at me. "Are you talking to me?"

"Yes. Are you a sociology student by any chance?" He nods, still confused by my approach. "I've noticed your band shirt. You don't happen to know a guy named Gaspar du Charbonneau?"

His eyebrows draw lower in recognition. "Why?"

I assume that's a "yes", but have to blink away tears before I'm able to speak. "Do you know where he lives? I've got his number, but he's not picking up. He never does."

"Is this a joke?" For some reason, the guy is starting to get angry.

This was a bad idea. "No, it's not. Look, I just really need to talk to him. It's important. I need to make sure he got home all right."

The guy still looks at me as if I've gone mad. He snorts, pulling a disgusted face. "He didn't." My heart misses a beat. "Gaspar died three weeks ago. He had a bike accident. Got run over by a van, right in front of the university."

I blink. "No."

"Yeah, didn't you hear about it?" Now that he's said his piece, he's calmed down a bit. "You're a bit late caring about his well-being, lady."

"Sorry." I don't know what else to say. Or what to think. "I'm sorry."

In a daze, I back away and slowly turn towards the entrance. A familiar man is waiting there for me. Officer Roubert.

He's not in uniform now, though he still seems to prefer sticking to a dark colour scheme. Hands stuffed in his pocket, he waits for me to make my way over. He greets me with, "I didn't want to tell you," obviously having overheard my conversation. "Not until I made sure I had the right guy."

"You knew?" I'm confused. How did he learn about Gaspar?

"I remembered hearing his name in the news." He pulls out his hands and clicks his tongue. "I'm sorry."

The words don't make sense. Nothing makes sense anymore. "I can't talk right now."

"Yeah, I figured. But please get in touch soon."

"Why? There's no longer a case, is there?" No, too close to what I don't want to think about.

Officer Roubert winces. "There is. But that's not why I'm here. I'm here for you, Alix. GoPol is always on the lookout for people like you." When understanding eludes me, he lowers his voice. "Ghost whisperers." His face softens. "I can see them too."

My mouth drops open. "You...?"

"Yes. But we can talk about it another time." He tries for another smile, but the situation stifles it. "You know where to find your friend now, don't you?"

I want to say no. That I've never been able to find Gaspar on my own. He's always come to me, but then I remember the principles of my talent and walk right out of the door.

Across from the university, at the corner of the street, I find Gaspar standing on the side of the road. The accident is still marked by a few wilted flower bouquets, burnt-down candles, and pictures weighed down by stones. Soon, it'll be gone. But for now, Gaspar is here.

"There you are!" He smiles widely at me, making my stomach lurch in agony. Oh, how I missed that smile for the last forty-eight hours.

Tears spring to my eyes. "And there you are." My voice breaks around the words.

Gaspar comes over to me, attempting to put his hands on my arms. "I was so worried about you when we were separated." When I shirk away from his touch, he lets his arms fall. "I came back for you, but you were gone. I didn't know whether you made it out alive or..."

I can't take it anymore. Not from him. "I did. But you didn't."

His face falls. "I—"

"You weren't even alive to begin with." I draw in a shaky breath, tears streaming down my cheeks.

"Alix..." Regret laces his voice.

I force out the words I don't want to say. "You're dead, Gaspar. You're nothing but a ghost."

# Afterword

P hew. What an emotional end to the first book. I hope you're okay. I'm as sad as you are about Alix and Gaspar, but of course, I knew Gaspar was dead from the moment we met him at the site of his accident.

Death isn't the end of the story in the case of *Parisian Ghosts*. Alix is a ghost whisperer, and now she's met another like her. Her newfound resolution of staying out of ghost business won't last very long, now that the Ghost Police are getting involved and her boyfriend turned out to be a ghost all along. And of course, there's the promise she gave Jacques de Molay. Never mind the sinister things le Chevalier d'Os has got planned for our heroine and the souls of Paris.

I hope you enjoyed this foray into the city of lights and the dark and mysterious city below. We will continue to explore Paris and all its illustrious locations. We will meet more famous people, try more French food, and further uncover secrets.

Thanks to my Story Seekers who have voted for Parisian Ghosts to be my next series. Whether you follow me on Facebook or via my newsletter, you're the reason I tell these stories.

For *Parisian Ghosts*, I tried something new and did a crowd-funding campaign. X amazing people have pledged their support and helped me develop the series. I hope you're happy with the end result. Thank you so much for believing in me, Alix, and Malou.

A special thanks go to Chris Rowan, who's my French adviser and treasured author friend, and also my chief beta reader for the series. Thank you so much for answering all my weirdly specific and unspecific questions and supporting the story before it even became a thing. Your own success inspires me. You're doing fabulous, man. Long may it continue.

Malou wants to thank Laura Greenwood for enabling hedgehogs to take over the book world and supporting her worm dominance with appropriate games, fun, and belly rubs. I promise Malou got every belly rub she deserved for collecting pre-orders, even if not all of them made it on the page.

A big thank you to all the FAKAs, some who supported me as beta readers, by pledging their support, or just cheering me on. You know who you are. Keep kicking ass. The same goes for all the beta readers who aren't authors but amazing detail-oriented readers. Love you!

Jackie, I wouldn't know what I'd do without our often daily Zoom sessions. Thanks for keeping me accountable, listening to all my woes, and helping to shape *Parisian Ghosts* into what it is today. I'm so glad I met you!

And, of course, thanks to all the wonderful amazing readers and followers on Facebook, TikTok, my newsletter, and wherever else I picked you up. You have made the lead-up to this series so enjoyable. Thanks for joining the Malou hype and making her the best pre-ordered hedgehog ever ;) See you all back for *Ghosts of the Crusade*!

Love, Janna

The adventure continues...

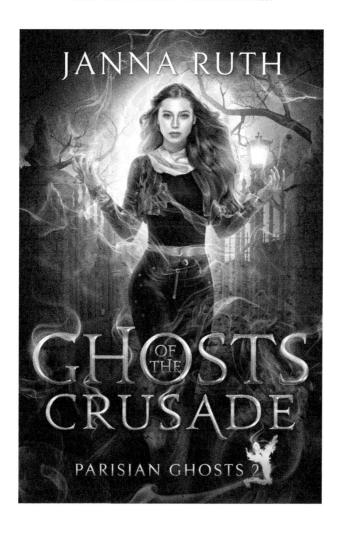

Book 2: Ghosts of the Crusade

# A Force of Nature (Spirit Seeker 1)

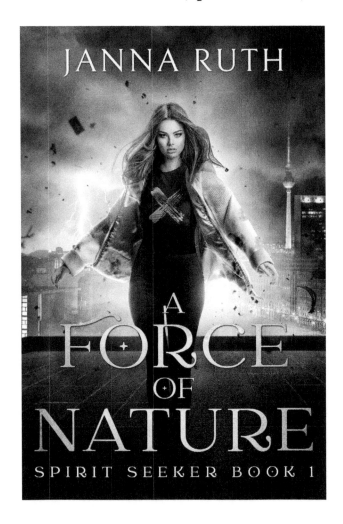

**A supernatural adventure through Europe**

# A Drop of Magic (Ashuan Greed 1)

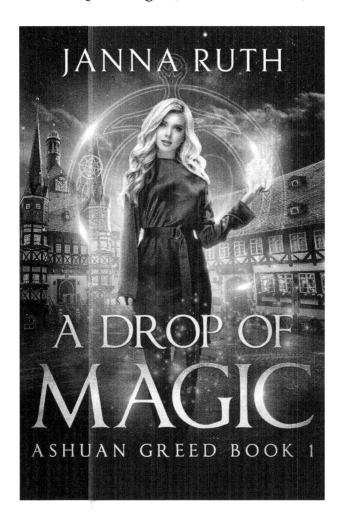

JANNA RUTH

A DROP OF
MAGIC

ASHUAN GREED BOOK 1

**Magic, Demons and High School Drama**

# About Janna Ruth

Once upon a time, Janna Ruth studied the plate boundaries of this world. Now, she's creating her own worlds. Born in Berlin, Germany, Janna lives in Wellington, New Zealand, writing both English and German books.

Janna's writing career kicked off when she won a writing competition for German publisher Ueberreuter. Her first self-published novel "Im Bann der zertanzten Schuhe" (Melody of Curse, coming in June 2022) went on to win the 2018 SERAPH for "Best Independent Title". She debuted in English with her witchy novella "Witching with Dolphins" in 2020 and has since published urban fantasy, YA sci-fi, and contemporary coming-of-age novels and series.

When Janna isn't writing, she has a plethora of hobbies, such as aerial acrobatics, cake decorating, drawing, reading, and anything crafty you can throw her way.

## Find out more about Janna and her books here:

www.janna-ruth.com